GARCÍA MÁRQUEZ
FOR BEGINNERS

Mariana Solanet

Illustrated by
Héctor Luis Bergandi

Orient BlackSwan

GARCIA MARQUEZ FOR BEGINNERS

ORIENT BLACKSWAN PRIVATE LIMITED

Registered Office
3-6-752 Himayatnagar, Hyderabad 500 029 (A.P.), INDIA
e-mail: centraloffice@orientblackswan.com

Other Offices
Bangalore, Bhopal, Bhubaneshwar, Chennai, Ernakulam, Guwahati, Hyderabad, Jaipur, Kolkata, Lucknow, Mumbai, New Delhi, Patna

Translated by Patricia Pitchon
Book Design: Renée Michaels
Cover Design: Bindia Thapar

Published by arrangement with
Writers and Readers Limited
P O Box 29522
London NI 8 FB

First published in India by
Orient Longman Private Limited 2004
Reprinted 2008
First Orient Blackswan impression 2010

ISBN 13: 978 81 250 2661 7
ISBN 10: 81 250 2661 4

Printed in India at
Glorious Printers
Delhi

Published by
Orient Blackswan Private Limited
1/24 Asaf Ali Road
New Delhi 110 002
e-mail: delhi@orientblackswan.com

Contents

Aracataca, 6 March 1927

He was born practically dead, rigid with the terrifying experience of suffocation and a long, difficult birth process. His halcyon days in the womb were shattered when, if he wished to live, he was impelled to take the hazardous journey through a dark, narrow, murky canal. What doubts seized him in that moment of panic and trepidation before he surrendered to the inevitable ordeal? He was blue when he was born, with a double loop of cord around his neck and his lungs nearly bursting as he took his first breath. He opened his eyes to his mother's look of complicity. He saw the other women around him. He had survived; there was nothing that could harm him now.

But he did not die, and in the arms of Francisca Cimodosea Mejía—**Aunt Mama**—one of the most influential women in his life, he was given the name **Gabriel José García Márquez**, or 'Gabito' to his friends. This wide-eyed boy did not want to miss a single marvel that this world had to offer. Had that not been so, his fabulous stories would never have been written. Nor would this book.

Gabriel García Márquez is now a king among writers, holding us spellbound in the magic he weaves. Today, there are in print about 30 million copies of this eminent Colombian's celebrated book, ***One Hundred Years of Solitude***—in almost every language you can think of. *Newsweek* called him the world's most important living writer—and this the man who didn't want to be news, but to go out and get it.

During his years as a reporter, he had dreamed of becoming a successful writer. But he had never imagined that he would attract such attention. The desolate characters he had created led him to unthought-of success and opened previously closed doors. Each of his books has sold millions of copies, and in his native Colombia, he has acquired hero status. Wherever he went he unleashed the passions of huge numbers of people. His readers loved him unconditionally, as fervently as a fan club.

Before we get into the story, let's take a deep breath, relax and look at some of the significant features of this man's life and character.

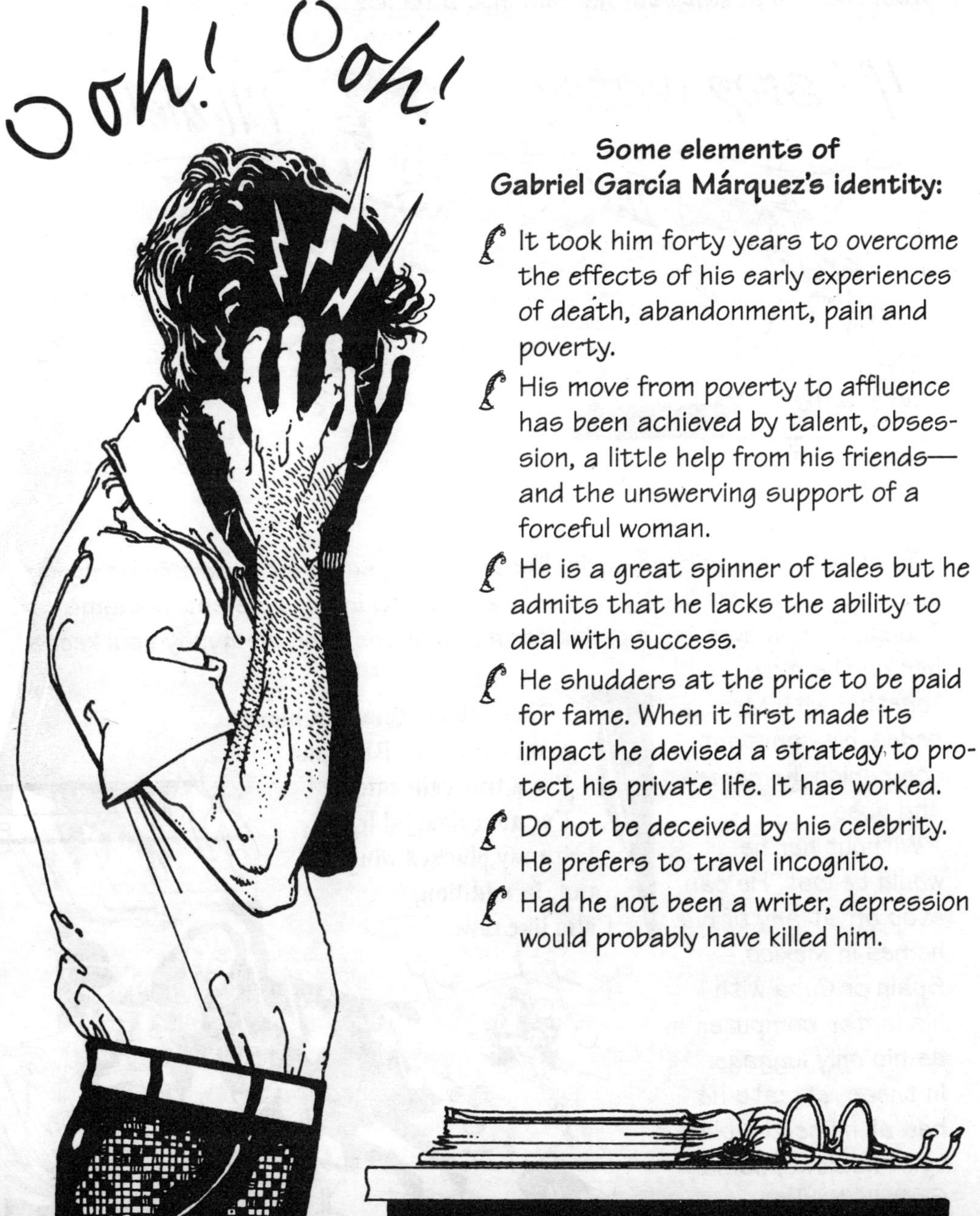

Some elements of Gabriel García Márquez's identity:

- It took him forty years to overcome the effects of his early experiences of death, abandonment, pain and poverty.
- His move from poverty to affluence has been achieved by talent, obsession, a little help from his friends—and the unswerving support of a forceful woman.
- He is a great spinner of tales but he admits that he lacks the ability to deal with success.
- He shudders at the price to be paid for fame. When it first made its impact he devised a strategy to protect his private life. It has worked.
- Do not be deceived by his celebrity. He prefers to travel incognito.
- Had he not been a writer, depression would probably have killed him.

He turned 74 in March 2001. He has been married for more than forty years to his one and only wife, **Mercedes Barcha Pardo**. They have two sons, **Gonzalo** and **Rodrigo**. He is also a grandfather. This King Midas of literature could retire with all the laurels he has won, but the mere prospect of inactivity throws him into a panic.

To dispel this panic, he works like an ox. His schedule is hellish. He rarely gives interviews. He barely has enough time to indulge his enthusiasms. Though he now lives in Colombia for most of the year, his gypsy soul keeps him on the move.

Together with Mercedes, his constant companion, he comes and goes.

Without her he would be lost. He can stop off at any of his homes in Mexico, Spain or Cuba with his laptop computer as his only luggage. In these retreats he has all he needs: plenty of windows, some Scotch, books, music...

In these locations, he organises workshops for young writers, journalists and scriptwriters, which he pays for and occasionally runs. Why would this Colombian Nobel prize-winner, with all his money, prestige and fame, devote a whole week to leisurely conversation with a dozen apprentices? His life and work draw on memories and reminiscences; they are the base material from which he recycles emotions.

Nothing on earth pleases him as much as telling stories. Taking on the role of sage, he deploys all his charm. At such times, one sees the real García Márquez: a man of the Caribbean, an anti-intellectual, a man who conveys his knowledge with a dollop of humour—taking the solemnity out of life.

Gabo likes to organise public events whenever he wants to meet his readers without the intervention of publishers. He did so in 1996 when he introduced them to extracts from his autobiographical work in a four-day seminar at Guadalajara University. In the Mexican capital on a Saturday in the spring of 1998, Gabo read the first chapter of his memoirs—or 'anti-memoirs' as he liked to call them—to an audience of about 2,000. They filled the colonial rooms and gardens of the Colegio Nacional and included students of literature, autograph hunters, fetishists and the simply curious. He had set himself the task of writing his memoirs after finishing **Love in the Time of Cholera**, as a way of 'keeping his hand in' between two novels.

The crux of the *Memoirs* is an attempt to remedy a kind of rebellion by his memory, which in recent times torments him even more than the invasion of his private life.

The point of departure for **Living to Tell It** is Gabo's return to Aracataca at the age of twenty-five, when he discovered a way forward for his writing. The collection of reminiscences, planned in six volumes, will be published whenever they are finished.

My mother asked me to accompany her to sell the house. She had arrived that morning from the distant village where she lived with the family and didn't have the slightest idea where to find me. Enquiring here and there among acquaintances, she was told to look for me at the Librería Mundo or in the nearby cafés, where I went every day at noon and at six in the evening to chat with my writer friends. She was warned, 'Go carefully, for they are dangerous madmen'.

The memoirs give readers glimpses of as many lives as the magus from Aracataca wishes to tell us about. For his most faithful devotees, those familiar with his books, this first reading might have had a certain déja vu quality to it. Though he does carefully guard his own intimate world in his memoirs, he does not hide the central themes that nourished the various stages of his life.

All his works start from a strong image. He recalled one from his childhood in Aracataca when an old man took a young boy to see ice for the first time. From this was born the first sentence of *One Hundred Years of Solitude*, which is possibly the most acclaimed work of world literature in the second half of the twentieth century.

He became a star reporter in his homeland after writing a series of articles about **Luis Velasco**, a sailor who spent ten days adrift on a raft without food or drink.

Tell me everything, right from the beginning...

We had been in Mobile, Alabama for eight months when on 22 February, we were told that we were to return home to Colombia.

In 1955, the daily newspaper *El Espectador* sent him to Europe to cover the Geneva summit. After an eventful flight to Paris, he boarded the train for Switzerland.

The grass is the same as that seen from the window of an Aracataca train.

So much flying, so much drinking, so many changes of transport, only for the grass to remain exactly the same as in Aracataca!

So, who is this man who said that he began writing, '...only so that my friends should love me more...' and ended up becoming the most potent symbol of Latin American literature? When asked to define himself, he says:

Caribbean Culture

The Caribbean is a country in its own right. As a region, it encompasses the Atlantic coasts of Colombia, Venezuela and Panama, up to the Gulf of Mexico, the South of the United States, and including the Antilles. It is not a mere place on a map. It possesses a unique cultural identity, with a colourful mosaic of nationalities, peoples, traditions, legends and faiths. It shows one of Latin America's faces: that of African and Amerindian roots, with features from Iberia, Arabia, as well as Nordic and Anglo-Saxon Europe. Its inhabitants, whose character tends to be upbeat, expansive and teasing, identify strongly with their music, with lively dancing and endless carnivals.

In the Caribbean, things happen that seem outlandish, fantastic, even supernatural to other people. That fact should be stranger than fiction in Latin America surprises only those unfamiliar with these parts. In the Caribbean everything is heightened and miracles are accepted as part of everyday life.

150 Years Before, in the Same Region

The writer's great-grandfather, **Nicolás del Carmen Márquez,** came to Riohacha at a young age from his native Castille, accompanied by his widowed mother. It is said that ten days later he met **Simón Bolívar,** when, in 1830, the Liberator undertook his journey of death on the Magdalena River. In that legendary city of pirates and smugglers, Nicolás fathered a number of illegitimate children. He became an esteemed jeweller before marrying **Luisa Josefa Mejía.** They had four children. The eldest, **Nicolás Ricardo Márquez Mejía,** was Gabo's grandfather. Because of the family's poverty, he was raised by his maternal grandmother along with his beloved cousin, **Francisca Cimodosea Mejía.** She was the 'Aunt Mama' who kept a close eye on the writer's mother's admirers and would later watch over the sleeping Gabo.

At 17, Nicolás Ricardo Márquez returned to the city of his birth, where his father taught him the art of working with silver.

Like father, like son. Grandfather Nicolás was yet another enthusiastic fornicator who would produce numerous illegitimate offspring. The luscious setting of the tropics seems to work like a powerful aphrodisiac.

At twenty-one, Nicolás married **Tranquilina Iguarán Cotes**, the illegitimate daughter of a half-sister of great-grandfather Nicolás. They were cousins, like José Arcadio and Ursula in *One Hundred Years of Solitude*. They had three children: Juan de Dios, Margarita and **Luisa Santiaga**, Gabito's mother. None was born with two heads! In Barrancas, Nicolás became a master jeweller, working in silver.

Later, they bought a farm in the foothills of the Sierra Nevada of Santa Marta. Nicolás grew mostly sugar cane to distil *chirrinche*, an anise-flavoured liquor, which was then bootlegged.

Barrancas was a close-knit and tranquil community; the people tilled the slopes of the Montes de Oca and grew corn, beans, yucca, plantain, coffee and sugar cane.

Those were days of peace and prosperity. They did not last. Two misfortunes were to shatter the lives of the Márquez Iguaráns.

The first misfortune was the **War of a Thousand Days.** This tragic and bloody conflict was to cause 100,000 deaths and severely damage Colombian production, trade and communications. It followed a century of civil conflicts—struggles between two models of society: one Conservative, with support from the clergy, the landowners and the armed forces; the other Liberal, with its roots in the culture of Garibaldi and French radicalism.

As a matter of principal and also for adventure, Nicolás Márquez enlisted in the army of the legendary Liberal leader, **General Rafael Uribe Uribe**, who led the forces that rose up against the Conservative government. He obtained the rank of revolutionary colonel. In some battles he had to face his wife's relatives and his two eldest illegitimate sons.

He was put in front of a firing squad.

At his typewriter, many years later, Gabo was to remember the thousand and one anecdotes told to him by Grandfather Nicolás. The War of a Thousand Days, which ended with the revolutionaries' defeat, was the model used for the wars of Colonel Aureliano Buendía in *One Hundred Years of Solitude* and other works. However, the appearance of the colonel was unlike that of the portly Nicolás and was more like that of General Uribe Uribe, who was gaunt and austere of character.

The second event that was to change the fortunes of the Márquez Iguaráns occurred six years after the ferocious civil conflict had ended. It was an event that would make a deep impression on the future writer.

Nicolás Márquez was well-liked and respected in Barrancas. He was a happy man until the memorable day of 19 October 1908, when he was obliged to take part in a duel and kill his old friend and companion-in-arms. This young man was **Medardo Romero Pacheco**, the illegitimate son of Medarda Romero and Nicolás Pacheco.

Popular gossip says that 'that whore, Medarda, is rolling in the hay with that Arcadio'.

While Nicolás and his friends chatted in the plaza, someone remarked for the umpteenth time: 'I met that Medarda last night. I'll bet she was coming from seeing Arcadio...'

Nicolás thought to himself, 'It must be true!'. Medarda complained to her son that 'Colonel Márquez... has wronged me.'

That's how life was in the town. People followed the social conventions inherited from the Guajiro Indians. These included a strict code of honour, like the Sicilian Mafia's *vendetta*. Medarda pestered her tall, broad-shouldered son until he had no choice but to satisfy her lust for revenge against the colonel. One afternoon, Medardo challenged him, hurling all kinds of insults at him...

Medardo continued with his provocations, and the colonel prepared for the inevitable duel. He sold the farm and paid up his debts. Finally, at five o'clock on a grey afternoon, as a mist descended...

Medardo arrived dressed in white linen, presenting a perfect target for the colonel...

The colonel told his wife what had happened and then gave himself up to the mayor. He admitted the charges at the hearing, but added: 'I killed Medardo and I'd do it again!'. The ghost of Medardo was to haunt the colonel for the rest of his life, just as the ghost of Prudencio Aguilar haunts José Arcadio in *One Hundred Years of Solitude*.

Colonel Márquez was sentenced to one year in the Santa Marta jail. Thus began an exodus for the family which was not resolved until nearly two years later in 1911, with the passage of Haley's Comet marking its end. Nicolás was appointed to the post of departmental tax collector in Aracataca, a village on the north coast. The family arrived in a brand new yellow train, to settle in a land that had not been promised them.

Only months after the family bought a house, Margarita, the eldest daughter, died of typhoid fever at the age of twenty-one. Burdened by so much death, the colonel was never the same man again. The loss of his favourite daughter deepened his melancholy. To cap it all, he was destined to spend the rest of his life waiting for a war pension that never came. Gabito would be the only light in the colonel's autumn and the grandfather would be the most influential figure in the writer's life.

Aracataca ('river of the chief') was founded by the Cataca Indians. It had been a peaceful village, trading farm produce and handicrafts with its neighbours, until the excesses of alcohol and smallpox ruined its culture. The colonisers took advantage of this situation and seized the land. During the regime of **General Rafael Reyes** in the early twentieth century, large-scale banana plantations brought sudden prosperity to the Magdalena valley. In 1905, the **United Fruit Company** established itself in the village and brought an endless stream of immigrants into the area. The stories and legends of the banana bonanza attracted adventurers, smugglers and whores like a magnet. It was called the '**leaf storm**'. Dance halls, brothels and gambling dens opened, and the town became known as a hotbed of sin, free spending and dissipation.

It is said that there was a tidal wave of money, that voodoo and witchcraft were rife and that families arrived bringing their ancestors' bones with them. Around that time, the first parish priest was brought in. He was **Pedro Espejo** and was better known for performing certain miracles than for his pastoral work.

Those years were also marked by violence. It began with the massacre of innocent locals from the coast by gangs of delinquents. But when an outsider from Antioquia in the interior killed a native, the traditional rivalry flared into popular vengeance. Aracataca fell into a two-year period of vigilante justice. Innocence had been lost. When a plague of locusts appeared in 1914, it brought to mind the wrath of God. It would not be the only Biblical retribution.

Aracataca was declared a municipality in 1915 in an attempt to contain the chaos. For the first time, the town was given the authority of a mayor. The people were divided by social status. The engineers and the American managers grouped together and maintained an American way of life. They lived in a neighbourhood with street lighting and associated only with the 'right' society—foreigners, company executives and the old colonels and generals who had prestige as local patriarchs. There was mutual disdain between the ordinary people and this social set.

Beyond the fence were the houses of the 'gringos'; houses equipped to fight off the heat and the insects, with porches where people played cards, swimming pools, tennis courts, green gardens and blondes who drove the latest convertibles.

In Aracataca, the colonel served as municipal treasurer and once again devoted himself to working silver. The upper-class world of the Márquez Iguarán family in Aracataca is reflected in the novels of García Márquez, where the Buendías are portrayed as the most important family in Macondo.

One day in 1924, at the height of the banana bonanza, **Gabriel Eligio García Martínez** arrived in the town. He was the new telegraph operator and was destined to be Gabo's father. He brought a letter of introduction to the colonel from a mutual friend.

The colonel not only received him cordially, but also invited him to supper and helped him to get established. Months later, when the young man wanted to court their daughter, Luisa, her parents were opposed to it. They regarded him as part of the leaf storm. Gabriel was born in 1901 in Cincé, Bolivar. This was considered a province of raucous, crazy people, very much in contrast to the Márquez Iguaráns. Luisa was the apple of the colonel's eye and he didn't look favourably upon this young man as a match for his daughter. Gabriel was illegitimate, dark-skinned, poor—and a Conservative too. But the colonel was to learn that Gabriel was his equal in his prowess with women.

One evening in 1924, Gabriel proposed marriage to Luisa. Aunt Francisca Cimodosea was close by, keeping watch.

Luisa could not meet Gabriel's deadline since her aunt never left them alone for an instant, but they arranged to meet the next day, after mass.

When the colonel found out what had been going on, he was so incensed that he refused to speak to the telegraph operator and banned him from the house. But such opposition only fanned the lovers' ardour and they found ingenious ways of overcoming all the obstacles. They managed to send each other covert messages arranging secret rendezvous. As time went by, Gabriel grew increasingly daring. One day he gave Luisa a handkerchief with some verses of his:

It was decided that the lovers had to be separated. Luisa and her mother would take a trip. What the parents didn't anticipate was that Gabriel had a telegraph operator as an accomplice in every town who would help him to keep in touch with his fiancée. Tranquilina only became aware of the futility of her efforts when, on arriving in Santa Marta, she spotted Gabriel, dressed in white from head to toe, waiting for his girl. His parents' embattled love affair was to inspire García Márquez's favourite novel, ***Love in the Time of Cholera***.

Luisa remained in Santa Marta with her brother. Meanwhile Gabriel requested a transfer to Riohacha. Luisa wrote to the town's curate, Monsignor Espejo, asking him to intercede with her parents. Reluctantly, they consented to the wedding, which was held on 11 June 1926. The groom was angry enough to forbid the bride's parents attending the wedding. The couple set sail in a schooner for Riohacha, the legendary city by the Caribbean that Sir Francis Drake had attacked in the sixteenth century.

When her parents discovered that Luisa was pregnant, they tried to rebuild the relationship. Gabriel stood his ground in spite of receiving gifts of fruit, candies, baby clothes etc. every week. He finally relented when his brother-in-law told him that Tranquilina was prostrated by the quarrel. Luisa returned alone to Aracataca to give birth in her parents' house.

On the sultry morning of Sunday 6 March 1927, while the colonel was at mass, death hovered over the house. The birth was protracted, and the mother grew weak through loss of blood. Finally, they called **Juana de Freites**, an exiled Caracan who, with her breathing exercises and magical massages, saved both mother and child from almost certain death.

The Land of Childhood

It was months later before Gabriel Eligio met his son. The couple returned to Aracataca for a short while before moving to Barranquilla in January 1929. By then they had a new-born second son. Gabriel Eligio now opened a pharmacy and devoted himself to his true calling: homeopathy.

In December 1928, there had been a **banana plantation massacre**, which led to the start of Aracataca's decline and revealed the town's underlying problems:

The banana plantation workers, together with union leaders, called a general strike in the zone, demanding improvements. In Cienaga they drafted a nine-point petition:

PETITION

- The establishment of general health insurance
- Compensation for workplace accidents
- Paid leave on Sundays and hygienic living quarters
- A 50% increase in wages
- The closure of commissariats
- Payment weekly, not fortnightly
- An end to individual contracts and compliance with collective contracts
- A hospital for every 400 workers
- A doctor for every 200 workers, expansion of the workers' camps, with better hygiene.

Alberto Castrillo • Erasmo Coronel
Eduardo Mahech
Workers' Union of Magdalena

Although the demands were justified, the strike was doomed before it had even begun. As happened in Central America and the Caribbean, the United Fruit Company wielded political power under its economic banner. In a similar situation in Colombia, the company argued that it had no workers under contract and their demands were, therefore, invalid. The company knew that it could count on the President's covert complicity in whatever actions it chose to take. Although Gabito was under two years old at the time of the massacre, it was to become a literary obsession. In *One Hundred Years of Solitude*, he recreated the fateful trap laid by the government for the workers: when they gathered at the station in Cienaga, the workers planned to march to Santa Marta to deliver their petition to the governor...

Over 3,000 people, including, women and children, filled the open space in front of the station. They thronged the adjacent streets, blocked by the army with rows of machine guns. José Arcadio Segundo was among the crowd that had been gathering at the station from daybreak on Friday.

When Jose Arcadio Segundo came to, he was lying face up. It was pitch black. He realized that he was in an endless and silent train. Then he discovered that he was lying on dead bodies.

Trying to escape the nightmare, José Arcadio Segundo dragged himself from car to car, and by the lightning flashing through the wooden slats as they passed sleeping villages, he could make out the dead bodies—of men, women and children. They would be dumped in the sea, like bunches of rejected bananas...

García Márquez grew up with the idea that the dead had numbered in their thousands. When he studied the records and discovered that there had been only seven people killed, he wondered what massacre it was that he had been told about. But by converting the bunches of bananas into dead bodies, he saw how the carriages could be filled in a way that seven bodies could never do. He revealed 'I said in the novel that there had been three thousand killed in the massacre, and thrown into the sea. That wasn't so. It was an invention'.

It was not *his* invention, though, but that of popular imagination. After the shootings, the people turned against United Fruit. Two more incidents would precipitate the company's withdrawal from the region. One was the financial crash of 1929, which lowered export quotas. The other was the flood of 1932—another phenomenon that would fascinate García Márquez.

It rained for four years, eleven months and two days...

At his grandparents' request, Gabito lived in the big house in Aracataca. Such an arrangement was common in the Caribbean, especially among poor families. His parents had another ten children, sometimes in conditions of extreme poverty. Their first-born grew up in a house dominated by women and haunted by ghosts. Childhood would be his most fertile literary inspiration, an essential source for everything he wrote.

My childhood was full of strange wonders. My grandparents seemed like fabulous beings to me. They had an enormous house, full of ghosts. They were people with great imaginations and superstitions. In every corner of the house there were dead people, and intimations of the past. After six in the evening you couldn't roam around the house.

It was a world of wonder and terror, full of cryptic conversations.

In spite of Gabito having become the focus of everyone's affection, there was a seed of loneliness in his heart, perhaps planted by his mother's absence. It left him with the pain of abandonment and the emotional emptiness caused by that early separation. A meeting with his mother took place when he was three and a half. She came to the joint baptism of Gabito and his earth-eating sister, Margot, in December 1930.

She embraced me and I was quite frightened because I felt that I did not love her the way you should love a mother. That's my first memory of her.

That was the beginning of 'the most serious relationship of my life', as García Márquez himself would put it years later. Until then, his mother had been a composite made up of pieces of grandmother Tranquilina and his aunts.

GRANDMOTHER TRANQUILINA was a spare and dynamic woman with grey hair, whose cataract-clouded eyesight did not stop her supervising the kitchen and making the bread.

ELVIRA CARRILLO, Aunt Pa, was the illegitimate daughter of Colonel Márquez and Manuela Carrillo. She had come to Aracataca when she was twenty, and was well received by Tranquilina, who adopted her and loved her like a daughter.

FRANCISCA CIMODOSEA MEJÍA, Aunt Mama, was the great matriarch of the house. An untiring and imaginative woman, she was also the person that the town turned to for advice and guidance.

WENEFRIDA MÁRQUEZ, Aunt Nana, was the colonel's sister and soul mate. Even though she lived in another house with her husband, she exercised her authority just as the other women did.

Coming from La Guajira, a land of sorcerers, Indians and smugglers, Tranquilina acknowledged no borderline between the living and the dead. She spent her day giving orders, singing and speaking absurdities as she moved from one end of the house to the other. Gabito never ceased his demands and questions. Even when she answered him with some ridiculous statement, her poker-faced delivery made her grandson believe it all.

When the grandson became unmanageable, Tranquilina would lose her usual calm, exclaiming, 'Damn, what a nuisance that child is!' But she knew just how to control him. At night, she would tell him ghost stories and sing songs relating tales that she made up.

At night all my grandmother's fantasies, evocations and omens came to life. That was my relationship with her: a sort of invisible cord through which we both communicated with the supernatural universe. By day, this magical world fascinated me; by night it terrified me.

For Tranquilina, any natural event had a supernatural interpretation.

If a butterfly flew in the window, she would say, 'a letter is coming!'

If the milk boiled over, it was, 'We must be careful. Someone in the family is sick'.

Meanwhile, Aunt Francisca took care of Gabito and his younger sister Margot, who also lived with them. She bathed, fed and dressed them, took them to church, helped them with their homework and watched over them as they slept. Sometimes she tried to make Tranquilina face reality:

But Tranquilina was on a different wavelength, using her superstitions to protect the family. She made sure that she put the children to bed before the souls started roaming. If there was a funeral procession and the children were in bed, she made them sit up so that they wouldn't die with the passing body. Aunt Francisca had her own quirks too. Once, in bed with kidney trouble, she asked Aunt Pa to embroider a shroud and set up an altar to say the novena for her when she died.

Being the only males in this matriarchy, the sexagenarian grandfather and his grandson became close friends and accomplices. García Márquez loved his grandfather with a kind of visceral emotion. The elderly colonel would take him by the hand wherever he went, telling him stories of the war and of his sadness at having once killed a man. With him, the child got to know the outside world, the town and its characters.

He also met the colonel's friends, who talked about politics and the country's history. Well-mannered and precise in his speech, the grandfather was an oasis of calm in the midst of the anxiety his grandmother created. When she would spout some extravagance, his grandfather would take him aside, saying, 'Don't take any notice. It's just stuff women believe'.

He took Gabo bathing in the cold, crystal-clear streams, flowing down from the Sierras, in the middle of the plantations. The stones were white, polished and as large as prehistoric eggs...

One afternoon, Gabito came home and said that he had seen some fish that were as hard as rocks in the banana company's commissariat.

His grandfather took him to the street corner where there was a crate of red snappers. He opened the crate and showed him the wonder of ice—in the hottest town in the world. This was a memory that García Márquez would treasure among many others. He loved to recall the trips together to the islands of Curaçao and Aruba, where the colonel bought perfume and silk shirts that had to be smuggled back in.

In Aracataca, there lived the strangest people, who would become characters in his novels.

In the midst of such a world, the taciturn Gabito didn't have the slightest interest in learning to read and write. His great passion was drawing.

He learned to read and write at the Montessori School in 1935, when he was eight The school was founded by **Rosa Elena Fergusson**, his first teacher, who passed on to him—like a virus—her enthusiasm for the Spanish poetry of the so-called 'Golden Century'.

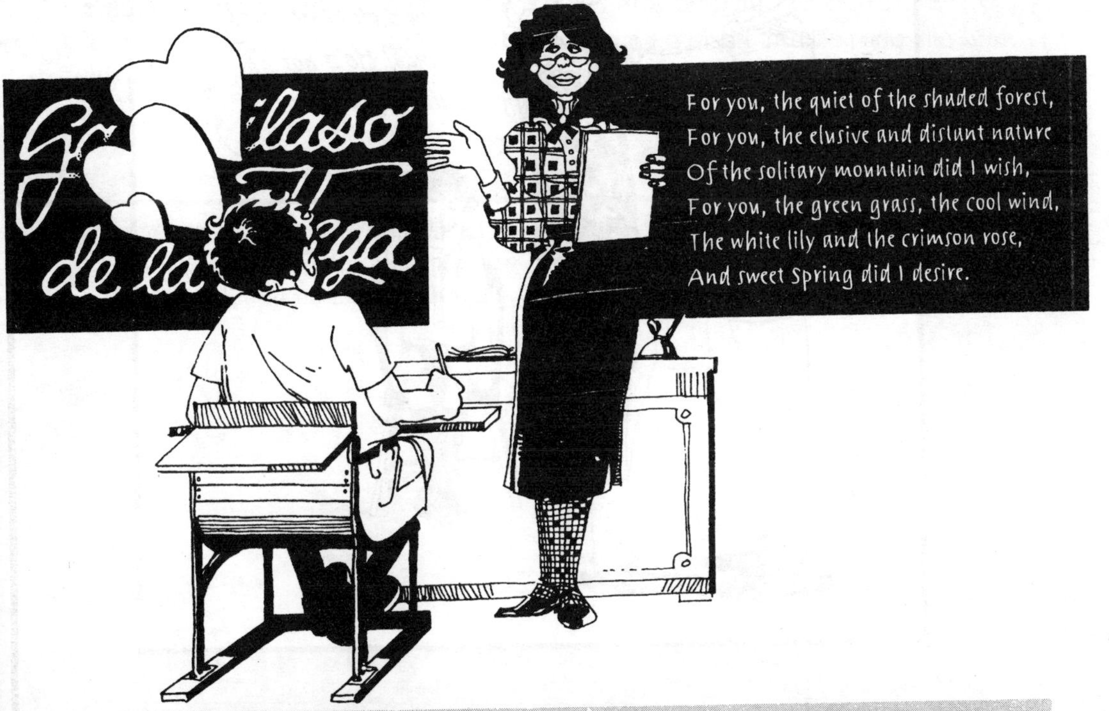

> For you, the quiet of the shaded forest,
> For you, the elusive and distant nature
> Of the solitary mountain did I wish,
> For you, the green grass, the cool wind,
> The white lily and the crimson rose,
> And sweet Spring did I desire.

One day, rooting around in the room where his grandparents kept odds and ends and mementoes Gabo found a book with no cover. It was Scheherazade's narration of the *Thousand and One Nights*. She told stories in the same deadpan way as his grandmother. From that moment, reading fascinated him more than playing, eating or painting. Later he read **Charles Perrault**, the **Brothers Grimm**, **Alexandre Dumas**, **Emilio Salgari** and **Jules Verne**.

In 1934, while Gabito was still attending primary school, his parents returned to live in Aracataca. He met his father on 1 December. He was seven years old, his father thirty-three. The García Márquez family rented a house close to the grandparents. Gabriel Eligio set up another pharmacy and got a licence to practice homeopathy.

In December 1936, the family moved once again. They went to Cincé, Gabriel Eligio's birthplace, in order to find better work. He took his two eldest children to meet their paternal grandmother for the first time. Gabito would never again see his beloved grandfather in Aracataca, for he died of pneumonia three months after his grandson had left. At ten, Gabito was no longer a small child.

In Aracataca, the wind would sweep everything away. At the time, nobody knew that this timid, phobic and solitary child felt the stirrings of a rudimentary anger. It would be fifteen years before he would face the ruin and desolation of the country of his childhood. He would then write about it in a way that would make the world take notice.

The Precocious Child

Gabito's return to the paternal household came as a relief to his mother. He was more than a son to her, he was an ally, someone she got on well with, whom she could count on to to be concerned about domestic problems—which were neither few nor pleasant. Things did not go well for the García Márquez family in Cincé and, around 1938, they returned to Barranquilla, where matters became even worse. There were a couple of very bad years when Gabito had to try hard to earn a few pesos in order to contribute to the home's precarious economy. Thanks to a steady hand, he landed his first job making posters for the corner store.

His first stroke of luck came on the day he won 25 pesos for painting a poster for a bus company. It was enough for a feast and some furniture, just at the time when the seventh child was about to be born. This was not a happy time for Gabito. He felt like a stranger in his parents' house. He had a warm and trusting relationship with his mother, but there was a mutual lack of understanding between him and his father.

When he began living with his parents, he brought with him a strong image of his grandfather as his role model. He didn't know how to relate to his father, who was the antithesis of the colonel. They were different in every way: in character, sense of authority, in how they related to their children, and their views on life. It would be years before Gabito would learn of their long-standing rivalry.

The conflict between father and son was always present, but never came to a head, because Gabito withdrew into himself and blotted the situation out most of the time. His father saw him as the old colonel's spoilt child and a 'liar'. He was right but didn't realise that in his son's innate capacity to spin a tale lay his greatest potential.

Gabito dramatised a little. His father was harsh, but not a really bad guy. He too had had a difficult upbringing. His own mother was only fourteen when he was born and his real father—a married man with five children—never cared about him. And anyway, Gabito's grandfather had been no saint himself.

In 1939, his father's wanderlust took them to Sucre. Gabo had inherited his grandfather's practical nature and he took care of all the details of the move. At twelve, he behaved like an adult. They lived in that isolated community for twelve years. The four youngest García Márquez children were born there, and the family experienced its first period of peace and relative happiness. In January 1940, Gabo went away to secondary school as a boarder, first in Barranquilla and later in Facatativá. He only came home for the holidays, and his brothers' memory of him is of a skinny, solitary boy who spoke little and read a lot. Some of his novels and stories are set in Sucre. It was his point of contact with Caribbean culture, with dances, friends and relationships.

One day his father sent him with a message to the town's brothel. Little did he expect what awaited him...

Many of his characters, like him, feel terror at their sexual initiation.

After completing the first years of secondary school at the San José Jesuit School in Barranquilla, Gabo travelled to Bogotá in search of a scholarship in 1943. The journey, which he repeated a dozen times, proved to be one of the most fascinating of his life. The boat, like Mark Twain's, took a week to paddle its way up the Magdalena River to Puerto Salgar at the foot of the Eastern Andes. Gabo travelled with other boys from the coast and, together, they sang *boleros* and *vallenatos* to earn a few pesos.

This enchanted journey was a source of nostalgia. The Magdalena became the river of love in *Love in the Time of Cholera*, the river of death in *The General in His Labyrinth* and the river of life in *Press Notes*, where he writes:

...it passed at night like an illuminated village and left a scattering of music and dreams in the sedentary villages of the river bank.

When the riverboat party reached Puerto Salgar, they resumed their journey on the train as it chugged up the mountain range. There was a man on the boat who always seemed to have a book in his hands. He asked Gabito if he would do him a favour and write down the words to one of the *boleros* for his girlfriend in Bogotá; he had already learned a bit of the melody.

The afternoon that Gabo arrived in the 'city of the cops' for the first time, he remembers as the saddest of his life. It was hard to breathe in the high mountain air, and from the tram car Bogotá seemed 'remote and mournful!'. There was a striking contrast between his Caribbean world and that of the Andes.

On the following day, he was standing in line in front of the Ministry of Education...

It was his lucky day. The man intrigued by the love song on the boat was a young lawyer from the coast and the national director of scholarships. He told Gabo that if he got a good result in his exam, he could have his scholarship without any further paperwork.

Gabo spent his final years of secondary school in Zipaquira, a small colonial town, fifty kilometres northwest of Bogotá. He described the Liceo National de Varones as being like 'a convent with no heating and no flowers!'. In fact, it wasn't that bad. Every evening, a teacher read aloud a chapter from **The Magic Mountain**, **The Three Musketeers**, **Madame Bovary**, **The Count of Monte Cristo** or some other classic novel. Thanks to the school and the progressive teachers who guided his reading, he fell in love with literature. At weekends, he would shut himself in and read his way through the library.

He was no longer so aloof or solitary. In his fourth year he would escape at night with his companions to visit their girlfriends in the town. On holidays the heat, the scent of guavas, the *vallenato* ballads and the reading he did in the shade of mango trees revived both body and soul.

At a students' dance, a thirteen-year-old girl captivated him. Her name was **Mercedes**. She was the eldest daughter of the Barcha Pardos, friends and neighbours of his parents.

The **'Piedra y Cielo'** (Stone and Sky) poetical movement was in vogue. **Carlos Martin**, the group's youngest member, was the headmaster of the school. He introduced Gabo to the work of **Rubén Darío**, whose childhood had much in common with his own.

He wrote his first stories and poems under the stimulus of his Spanish teacher **Carlos Calderón Hermida**, who guided him to good books: the classics—Homer, Virgil, Sophocles, Dante, Shakespeare, Tolstoy—as well as Spanish literature of the Golden Century and Colombian literature. Every time he swore, Gabo's 'punishment' was to write a story. The first was called 'Obsessive Psychosis' and had a Kafkaesque cast, though Gabo had not yet read the author of *Metamorphosis*. His story is about a girl who turns into a butterfly.

In 1947, to please his father, Gabo registered at the university in Bogotá to study law. But it was not to be. He was bored in class and spent most of his time elsewhere. He met other students in cafés who were as fanatic about literature as he was and they exchanged poems. With his local friends he found his first literary group and band of companions which included **Camilo Torres,** the future guerrilla priest, as well as **Gonzalo Mallarino, Luis Villar Borda** and **Plinio Apuleyo Mendoza**.

With 700,000 inhabitants, Bogotá boasted of being 'the Athens of America'. It had the pretension of being a Castillian town but, although psychologically it still had one foot in colonial times, it also copied English styles. It was nearly 2,700 metres above sea level, and had many churches, convents and literary cafés. Gabo already sported a moustache, long hair and a spidery signature. With his Cuban suits and loud ties, he cut a discordant figure. One day, Luis Villar Borda introduced him to Plinio Apuleyo Mendoza, who would become his companion in his journalistic adventures.

Gabo was still on the margins and without compass in a city where the cold and the loneliness were killing him. He felt superfluous, foreign everywhere away from the Caribbean.

He lived in a modest boarding house where he shared a room. On Saturdays, to escape melancholy, he would organise boisterous parties with his friends from the coast. Among them was **Clementino Gentile Chimento,** the model for the deceased Santiago Nasar in *Chronicle of a Death Foretold.*

He killed time on Sundays by riding on the trams that had circular routes. For just five cents these allowed him to clatter round and round the city while he read poems like one possessed. At this time, he came across the book that rekindled his interest in novels: Franz Kafka's **Metamorphosis,** translated by someone called **Jorge Luis Borges.**

The next day, he sat down and wrote 'The Third Resignation', a story in which the influence of Kafka was very apparent. According to Gonzalo Mallarino, it was also 'an autobiographical parable'. It tells the story of a boy of seven who, after dying of typhoid fever, remains for 18 years as a living corpse while his body reaches the age of twenty-five in the same coffin. While his mother takes care of him, he undergoes three successive deaths. The character's greatest misfortune is that his mind remains lucid while he tortures himself about his destiny.

His body was rigid and the decomposition had already begun. He was putrefying.

Soon they'll take me to sleep through my second death with the other dead ones. But I might not be dead, and if so, they're going to bury me alive!

Gabito's first real opportunity came when he read 'The City and the World' column in the daily paper *El Espectador*. The column was written by the author **Eduardo Zalamea Borda,** signed with the pseudonym 'Ulises'. At the end was this paragraph:

Though the literary production of our country's young people is not abundant, we especially welcome contributions from Colombian writers to the pages of our literary supplement. I eagerly await those from new poets and short-story writers who are unknown and ignored because of the lack of suitable avenues for publication.

Gabito sent in his story straight away. Two weeks later, to his great surprise, he spotted someone reading 'The Third Resignation' in print. When another two rather morbid stories were published, Zalamea Borda saluted García Márquez in the pages of El Espectador:

With Gabriel García Márquez, a new and notable writer has come into being. I do not doubt his talent, his originality, nor his desire to work.

The collection of stories, ***Eyes of a Blue Dog,*** published twenty years later, covered the period between 1948 and 1953, but the flames of the riots which were about to erupt throughout the city destroyed the originals of the early stories.

The Liberal leader, **Jorgé Eliecer Gaitan**, was shot dead on 9 April 1948. This incident was the spark which exploded into a spontaneous popular uprising that set fire to Bogotá. The wave of violence expanded to cover the entire country. The bloody episode, known as ***El Bogotazo***, left hundreds dead in the streets, which were devastated by fire, looting, and general mayhem. The long-standing struggle between the warring factions had intensified in the two years since the Conservative minority took power. Now it was at its height.

Fidel Castro, who would become one of Gabo's closest friends, was in Bogotá with other Cuban university students. They were organising the Congress of Latin American Students—which Gaitan had supported—in response to the 9th Pan American Conference, organised by Washington to counter the 'communist danger'. When Castro discovered that the police were on his trail, wanting to make him a scapegoat, he sought refuge in the Cuban embassy.

Because of *El Bogotazo*, the university was closed, and Gabo was left with no roof over his head, no studies and no literary cafés. So he returned to the Caribbean, where he became a journalist and began working on the great themes of his books, beginning with violence.

Gabo's first steps in journalism, in Cartagena and Barranquilla, coincided with the blackest period of the civil war known as ***La Violencia***, leading up to **General Rojas Pinilla**'s coup d'état. This period of his life on the coast was decisive in his education as a writer.

In May 1948, Gabo settled in Cartagena to resume his law studies, which he hated. Meeting up with a friend, the doctor and writer **Juan Zapata Olivella**, he asked to be introduced to **Clemente Manuel Zabala**, the editor of the recently-founded daily, *El Universal*. That is how he landed his first job as a journalist. Zabala introduced him thus:

> **Welcome to Gabriel García Márquez**
>
> In this new stage of his career, the scholar, writer and intellectual will use these columns to express the entire world of suggestion with which his spirited imagination, has impressed people and events.
>
> *El Universal*, 20 May 1948

Zabala was a master of his profession and he helped Gabo to find a style of his own by dint of repeated editing and rewriting.

Journalism would be his style school, helping him to develop his pieces into a literary genre.

His work on the coast helped Gabriel García Márquez to bring together literature and reality. This synthesis had been lacking while he was in Bogotá. In twenty months, he worked hard as a journalist, writing unsigned pieces while continuing to send stories to *El Espectador*. Wherever he went, Gabo sought out a circle of friends and mentors.

At that time, he began an interminable book—***La Casa*** (The House)—written on long strips of newsprint that he lugged everywhere with him to read to friends. They dubbed it 'the tome'.

In this atmosphere, his obsessions haunted him—his home, civil wars, the drama of Aracataca, solitude.

Years later, García Márquez acknowledged that this embryo of *One Hundred Years of Solitude* was 'too weighty' for his inexperience. From 'the tome', a number of offshoots eventually took form, among them his first novel, ***Leaf Storm***.

A love-hate relationship lasting twenty years linked him to the magical world of Cartagena. He would not forget the hunger, the miserable salary at the newspaper, or being rejected by a part of society because of his provincial origins. At the time, it did not seem to matter. He had a dream, an obsession. He wanted to be a writer, and was ready for anything.

In one of his earliest pieces, published in *El Universal* in May 1948, one finds the germination of the idea of Macondo as the universal village:

I could recall **The Thousand and One Nights**. I could say the spell for magic carpets that at the sound of a voice would carry a man over camels and mountains... I could speak of that anonymous rustic village which once passed on the shore of our journey. I could say that the village's belly was curved, pregnant with fruit, somewhat silent like a dormant mother. That beyond, uncurled, was the indispensable river. And that it flowed tamely, inhabited by bunches of fruit and children, as if the scene flowed only through the village memory.

As with Aracataca, Sucre, Valledupar and Barranquilla, Cartagena became part of Gabo's literary breeding ground. The city is the setting for two books of stories and the novels ***The Autumn of the Patriarch*** (1975), ***Love in the Time of Cholera*** (1985), ***The General in His Labyrinth*** (1989), and ***Of Love and Other Demons*** (1994).

Eager for new experiences, he slept very little. He lived by night. When the paper finally closed around dawn, he would leave for 'Matilde Arenales' house of rented beds' or the buzzing dock of the Bahía de las Animas, where the central market was. At other times, he would tour the old bars of the port. Over shots of cheap rum, he listened to the barflies' tales to flesh out his chronicles and stories.

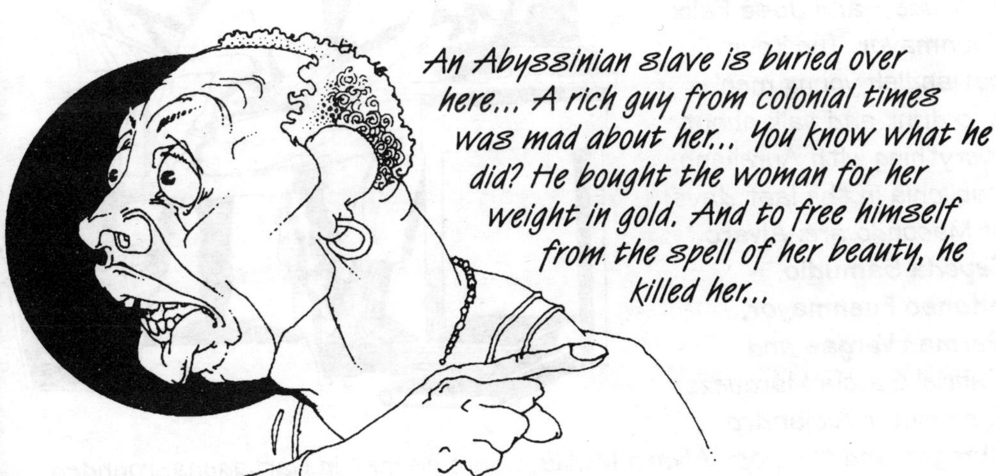

The first story would become 'Blacamán the Good, Vendor of Miracles'; the second one, he kept for forty-five years before including it in *Of Love and Other Demons.*

A Family in Literature

In September 1948, Gabriel met the crazy gang that would become his closest friends and who are known in the standard books on literature as the 'Barranquilla Group'. In ***The Smell of the Guava Tree,*** Plinio Apuleyo Mendoza writes:

> That group of outrageous revellers, bitten by the literary bug, that Gabriel met in Barranquilla, is now studied quite seriously at universities in Europe and the United States by specialists in Latin American literature.

The group was led by two older men, the Spanish Republican **Ramón Vinyes**—the Catalan 'sage' of *One Hundred Years of Solitude*—and **José Félix Fuenmayor**. The 'four outlandish young men' who drink and talk about everything with Aureliano Babilonia in the last days of Macondo are: **Alvaro Cepeda Samudio, Alfonso Fuenmayor, German Vargas** and Gabriel García Márquez. The painter **Alejandro Obregon** and the poet **Alvaro Mutis,** whom he met in Cartagena, rounded off the group. It would be decisive in his intellectual development. Later, in the story 'Big Mama's Funeral', Gabriel dubbed them 'the cock-breeders from La Cueva', a nod from afar to his 'brothers' in Barranquilla from the nostalgic Colombian, then based in Paris.

Because of overwork and an unhealthy lifestyle, Gabo contracted pneumonia. In March 1949, he returned to Sucre to convalesce. He used the opportunity to finish a first version of *Leaf Storm* and asked his friends in Barranquilla to send him something to read. He received three boxes with an assortment of recently-published books.

Back in Cartagena, his friend **Ibarra Merlano** was the first to read the typescript of the new novel, inspired by the story of Aracataca and his childhood, with narrative techniques learned from William Faulkner and Virginia Woolf.

I was excited to see that your topic is the same as Sophocles' in Antigone: the burial of a body in the face of the townsmen's opposition. I can see that you have the necessary gift to make it as a writer.

Well, you'll have to lend me Sophocles—and your knowledge of the Greeks—to guide me in my reading.

From then on, the Greek playwright became another of his essential masters.

In December 1949, García Márquez moved to Barranquilla, where the idea that the Caribbean is a country unto itself could be felt more radically. The city, a witches' cauldron that seemed like an outpost of hell, simmered in interminable heat, though people rarely lost their sense of humour or their festive spirit. Thanks to the arrival of a mass of immigrants—Jews, Germans, Frenchmen, Spaniards, Italians, Arabs—Barranquilla became the most cosmopolitan city in Colombia.

With its pungent smell of fresh fish and rotting guavas, Barranquilla—besides being the main river port on the Magdalena—was an oasis of peace and political tolerance in the middle of the country's violence and press censorship.

For the first time since he had first met her as a student, García Márquez saw a lot of Mercedes, whose family had now moved to the city.

1950 was a year of intense activity. At *El Heraldo*, he took charge of the international section, wrote a daily column—'The Giraffe'—and occasional leaders. Besides working on two novels, he edited *Crónica*, a sports/culture weekly. At the same time, he hung out with his circle of friends in bars and cafés. At night they would meet at a brothel to drink the best rum in town and watch the foreigners dance with 'girls who went to bed out of hunger'. The city's characters captivated him: taxi drivers, prostitutes, barmen in seedy joints, barbers, truck drivers, fishermen from the port...

For me, that was a time of amazement, and discovery, not only of literature, but of life. We would be drunk until daybreak, talking literature. Every night, at least ten books I hadn't read came up in conversation, and on the next day, they would lend them to me...

At dawn, he would arrive at the brothel-cum-tenement, where he rented a room. He became friendly with the girls, who lent him soap and shared their breakfast. His room became a salon for prostitutes and pimps where Gabo sang *vallenatos*. That strange house of prostitution passed, nearly intact, into ***The Autumn of the Patriarch***.

'...we saw the arches of the gallery with pots of carnations and astromelia leaves and pansies where the concubines' rooms had been... we thought it possible that over a thousand women had lived there with their swarm of seven-month babies; we saw the battle-field ravages in the kitchens, clothes rotting in the sun by the wash tanks, the open sewer shared by concubines and soldiers...'

Around this time, Losada, the Buenos Aires publishers, returned the manuscript of *Leaf Storm* with a devastatingly negative letter from **Guillermo Torres**, Borges' brother-in-law.

You will never become a good writer. It is better to devote yourself to something else...

He began a third version of the novel, which would be published five years later. He tried to write *One Hundred Years of Solitude*. He experienced each new book as another defeat, a part of a puzzle he just could not complete.

In January 1951 Gabo was in Cartagena, where his father was house hunting for the family's definitive move from Sucre. There he learned of the death of his friend **Cayetano Gentile Chimento** brutally murdered by his lover's family. It reminded him of Grandfather Nicolás' duel: outraged honour is cleansed with blood. Thirty years would pass before he sat down to write of this in *Chronicle of a Death Foretold*.

In literary reality, Sucre was the model for 'the town' which provided the setting for the *Chronicle of a Death Foretold, No One Writes to the Colonel, In Evil Hour*, and most of the stories of *Big Mama's Funeral*.

> In the town, suspicion and bad consciences reigned. Through lampoons posted on doors, anonymous allegations and accusations came and went.

In most towns on the coast, violence had ravaged society in an undeclared civil war with no clearly-defined factions. Political power won, the poor lost. There were conspiracies, and guerrillas in the hills. Many families escaped the towns.

Gabo had other urgent business. In Cartagena, the family was having a bad time once again. Their income was not enough to feed and educate so many children. The father needed help from his older children. Having political contacts, he landed them government jobs. Gabriel refused, and decided to come clean.

And so it continued. Upset by the death of his friend, the paternal curse had no effect on him. From Cartagena, he continued to send articles to *El Heraldo*, and also went back to his work at *El Universal*. To furnish the new house, Gabo got a loan from the newspaper, to be paid back by writing leaders, something he despised. The following year, his mother asked him to accompany her to Aracataca to sell his grandparents' house. He didn't know that this return visit would be decisive in terms of his writing.

The Revelation

Gabo was walking with his mother along a dusty, hot Aracataca street:

We passed through the town like passing a ghost town: there was not a soul on the street. I felt shaken. I had the feeling that what separated me from the town was not distance, but time. I was certain that the same thing was happening to my mother...

We went toward the pharmacy belonging to some old friends of the family. Inside, a woman was sewing. My mother asked her, 'How are you, good friend?' The woman looked up and recognised her. They embraced and cried without saying a word. I had the sensation that the entire town was dead, including the living.

In a letter to his friend from Aracataca, **Gonzalo Gonzalez** (*Gog*), at *El Espectador*, he described the state of ruination and solitude of Aracataca:

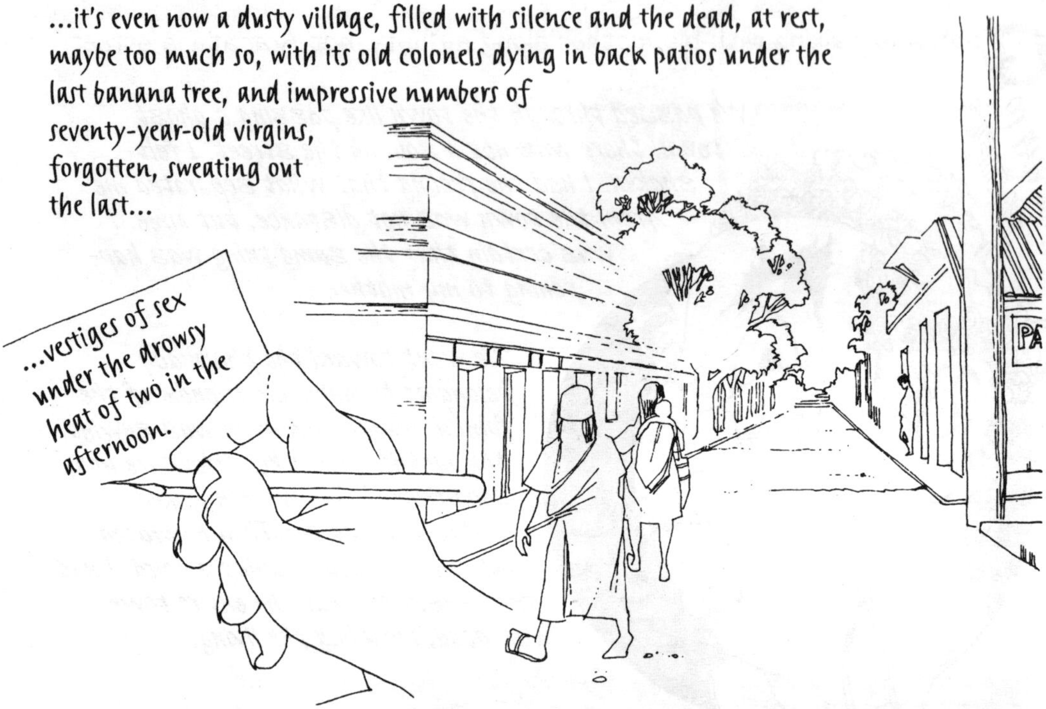

...it's even now a dusty village, filled with silence and the dead, at rest, maybe too much so, with its old colonels dying in back patios under the last banana tree, and impressive numbers of seventy-year-old virgins, forgotten, sweating out the last...

...vestiges of sex under the drowsy heat of two in the afternoon.

Something had just clicked. He now knew that any good novel must be a poetical transposition of reality, a coded world. If he wanted to find a literary solution for the story of demons that burned at the heart of his childhood, he would have to go back in search of his origins.

For four months, García Márquez journeyed back to his roots. Working as an encyclopaedia salesman, he roamed over the land of his ancestors. He went from town to town, collecting myths. With his friend **Rafael Escalona**—the popular composer of vallenato songs—he was moved to an in-depth study of the folklore and the history of each place.

Out walking one day, he met **Lisandro Pacheco**, the grandson of the man his grandfather had killed in a duel. Together they travelled through La Guajira to Riohacha. Pacheco introduced him to a number of his grandfather's illegitimate grandchildren. And he encountered other old and forgotten colonels.

> 'One Hundred Years of Solitude came out of Valledupar and La Guajira, because the folklore of Aracataca doesn't take more than half an hour to analyse. I took him everywhere and while I spoke and sang to him, he took notes. My friends complained that he asked too many questions. I would leave him absorbed in people and would go off with the musicians.'
>
> Told by **Escalona**, musician

The *vallenato* songs that tell stories in Grandmother Tranquilina's same natural style, are another of García Márquez's cultural reference points.

In Valledupar, he got hold of Ernest Hemingway's ***The Old Man and the Sea***. Here the length, structure and style allowed him to explore in depth the formal craft of the short novel.

He took the opportunity to meticulously re-read Virginia Woolf's ***Mrs. Dalloway***. A single paragraph at the beginning proved influential:

> ...But there could be no doubt that greatness was seated within; greatness was passing, hidden, down Bond Street, removed only by a hand's breath from ordinary people who might now, for the first and last time, be within speaking distance of the majesty of England, of the enduring symbol of the state which will be known to curious antiquaries, sifting the ruins of time, when London is a grass-grown path and all those hurrying along the pavement this Wednesday morning are but bones with a few wedding rings mixed up in their dust and the gold stoppings of innumerable decayed teeth.

It completely transformed my sense of time and allowed me to see in an instant the entire process of the ruination of Macondo and its final destiny.

Under the dictatorship of **General Gustavo Rojas Pinilla**, in 1954 García Márquez returned to Bogotá to work at *El Espectador*, Colombia's Liberal and democratic second paper. He was hired as a staff writer earning a good salary. His articles and film reviews reflected his socialist and anti-imperialist tendency (for a short while, García Márquez belonged to an underground cell of the Colombian Communist Party). For the first time, he worked as a reporter, a task he was passionate about. For his debut as the paper's special envoy, he was sent to cover the tragedy when the Media Luna building collapsed in Medellin. At his hotel, a terrible fear overcame him, similar to infantile terror.

This Tragedy Began 70 Years Ago
On Monday 12 July, just before seven in the morning, two boys, Jorge Alirio and Licirio Caro, 11 and 8, went out to chop wood. This was a job they did three times a week, using a small machete with a horn handle, worn down by use, after having breakfast with their father, Guillermo Caro Vallejo, 45. They lived with their mother and four other children in a house...

He decided to jump into the ring. He would learn to live with fear, as something congenital. His first story, in three parts, entitled 'Appraisal and Reconstruction of the Tragedy of Antioquia', made him a star reporter.

García Márquez's best-known piece of reporting was 'The Truth about My Adventure'. On 28 February 1955, eight crewmen of the Colombian Navy destroyer *Caldas* fell overboard and were given up for dead. Official reports pointed to a storm in the Caribbean as the cause. A week later, one of the shipwrecked men appeared on a beach, close to death. It was **Luis Alejandro Velasco**, a solidly-built 20 year old who had spent ten days without food or water aboard a drifting raft.

After becoming a national hero, the survivor approached the newsroom of *El Espectador* and offered to tell the true story of the accident, without official manipulation or propaganda.

My first surprise was that the sailor had an exceptional gift for storytelling, a good memory and sufficient dignity to laugh at his own heroism. In twenty daily six-hour sessions, we managed to reconstruct the concise and true story of his ten days at sea. My only problem would be to get the reader to believe it...

The next surprise, which was the best, came on the fourth day of work...

The truth was that when the ship veered suddenly in a heavy sea under high winds, some cargo on deck—having been badly tied down—became loose, and the eight sailors fell into the sea. This revelation shed light on three major errors...

First, it was forbidden to transport cargo on the deck of a destroyer. Second, the ship was carrying too heavy a load and was unable to manoeuvre to rescue the shipwrecked men. Third, the cargo consisted of contraband: refrigerators, TV sets, washing machines. It became clear that the story, like the destroyer, was also carrying a badly tied down political and moral cargo, something we had not expected.

The serialised story, was published on fourteen consecutive days during which time circulation doubled. The paper's publisher approached the reporter...

Told in the first person, the story's greatest challenge was to describe, without repetition or sensationalism, the ten empty and identical days the shipwrecked man spent adrift. On each day there was a unique event. The first day centred on the sailor's cosmic terror as the first Antillean night fell around him.

On the second night, planes flew overhead but did not spot him, and sharks appeared, punctually, at five in the afternoon.

According to García Márquez, the tale of adventure with its political charges unsettled the country, cost the shipwrecked sailor both glory and his career and condemned the journalist to an errant and nostalgic exile that finally felt much like being on a drifting raft.

In 1970, the story was published in book form under the title ***The Story of a Shipwrecked Sailor***. García Márquez gave Velasco the royalties from the Spanish edition, because 'there are books that do not belong to those who write them, but to whoever suffers them...' and he enjoyed those royalties until the author withdrew them twelve years later. In twenty-five years, over ten million copies have been sold worldwide. Nowadays, García Márquez is a world-famous writer. But in Colombia, in 1955, he was better known and appreciated for his reporting than for his fiction.

García Márquez published **Leaf Storm** himself, with the help of some friends. The story that casts light on Macondo as a mythic space was an exploration of the author's childhood. It was set in the house in Aracataca where he was born, during the wake for a doctor who had hanged himself. In monologues around the body, García Márquez tells the story of the town from its foundation up to the 1928 banana plantation massacres. The book centres around the doctor (the town is opposed to burying him) who had lived and died in absolute solitude. The three points of view are those of an old colonel (the faithful image of his grandfather), his daughter Isabel and the eleven year old grandson (Gabito?).

Macondo is the past, more than anything, and since the past must have streets and houses, a temperature and people, I made the image of this town—hot, dusty, rundown, ruined, with wooden houses and sheet metal roofs—very much like Faulkner's towns, because the United Fruit Company built it.

His dogmatic comrades from the Communist Party—who knew nothing about literature—managed to instil in him a terrible guilt complex, claiming, 'your novel denounces nothing, unmasks nothing'. This led him to think that in his next books he should deal with the country's immediate reality.

His success as a journalist was enough for *El Espectador* to decide to send him to Europe as a correspondent. For García Márquez, the trip was a wonderful opportunity to study cinema, broaden his horizons, and gain perspective. Before he left, the magazine *Mitos* published the story 'Monologue of Isabel Watching It Rain in Macondo', created from early drafts of *Leaf Storm*.

I saw the small garden, empty for the first time, and the jasmine against the wall, faithful to my mother's memory. I saw my father... his eyes sad, lost in the labyrinth of rain. I remembered the August nights, in whose marvellous silence one hears nothing more than the millennary sound of the Earth as it turns on its rusty axis in need of oil. Suddenly I felt overwhelmed by a crushing sadness...

The same crushing sadness invaded Mercedes just before Gabo's journey.

It will only be a few months, my love. When I get back, we'll get married. Tell me you'll wait for me...

You know I will. If you don't go, you'll blame me for the rest of your life.

Gabo's promise was kept, inexorably, like a mandate of destiny.

Rome, Summer of 1955

His first goal led him to Rome, the city of the actor and director **Vittorio de Sica** and the screenwriter **Cesare Zavattini**. He had a good salary, contacts and time to live at his own pace. He took with him a letter of introduction to the Argentinian film maker **Fernando Birri** who became both his guide and his accomplice. He registered at the Experimental Centre for Cinema, where he studied directing. For someone interested in the script as the basis for a film, the greatest attraction lay in the basement...

In the practical course on editing, he studied continuity, and also sent film reviews and articles back to Colombia. The five pieces he devoted to Pope Pius XII attest to his fascination with those beings who have supreme power. The pope makes cameo appearances in his novels and stories—and revealed the author's premonitory faculty.

'Big Mama's Funeral' tells of the Pope's fabled journey to Macondo in a black canoe.

Stifling in his tent, all night long the Supreme Pontiff heard the riot of the monkeys, startled by the passage of the crowds. On his nocturnal itinerary, the pontifical canoe had filled up with sacks of yucca, bunches of green bananas and crates of chickens.

His Holiness suffered that night, for the first time in Church history, the fever of sleeplessness and the torment of the mosquitoes. But the wonderful dawn over the dominions of the Grand Old Lady, the primeval vision of the kingdom of balsam and the iguana, erased from his memory the suffering of the journey.

In the Pope's Impossible Journey to a Colombian village, I described the president who receives him as bald and pudgy, so that he should not resemble the one then in office, who was tall and bony. In 1969, the pope came to Colombia and the president was like the one in the story.

Paris Was No Fiesta

In winter, he arrived in the cultural heart of Europe. He settled in the Latin Quarter, right in the tribal territory of so many Latin Americans who, wandering and in exile, had been banished from their countries. In Latin America, it was a time of dictatorships: Rojas Pinilla in Colombia, Manuel Odria in Peru, Anastasio Somoza in Nicaragua, Rafael Trujillo in Santo Domingo, Fulgencio Batista in Cuba, Pérez Jiménez in Venezuela, Pedro Eugenio Aramburu in Argentina.

Gabo took a room at the Hotel de Flandres, run by Madame Lacroix, where the poet **Nicolás Guillén** and Plinio Apuleyo Mendoza were also staying.

The cheques stopped coming, and a month later he had no way to pay his hotel bill. Fortunately, at critical junctures there was always a woman willing to lend a helping hand. Madame Lacroix allowed him to live in the attic on the seventh floor until he could pay her. He endured a period of extreme poverty surviving on small everyday miracles.

With its heart hardened by the affliction wars impose upon the people, Paris was not Barranquilla. After losing Indochina in 1954, it was then time for France to lose Algeria. Speaking only bad French, García Márquez survived by singing Mexican *rancheras* at a night-club, or collecting bottles and newspapers for a few francs. With his Turkish-looking face, he constantly had to keep out of the way of the police, who would beat him up whenever they mistook him for an Algerian.

He wrote looking inward. Throughout the night, he worked on the 'novel of lampoons', which would become *In Evil Hour* (1961) until one character compelled him to write a separate story. ***No One Writes to the Colonel*** (1958), opens with an image of extreme poverty.

...and noted that there was only a small spoonful. He took the pot from the stove, poured half the water onto the dirt floor, and with a knife scraped the inside of the tin until the last scrapings of coffee powder mixed with rust from the tin came loose.

The colonel, a decrepit and maniacal old man, waits every Friday for a war pension that never arrives. He lives with his wife in the ruins of a mortgaged house, in a town that was not Macondo. From his son Agustin—murdered a few months before at the cockfighting ring for distributing clandestine information—he inherits a fighting cock. The colonel decides to fatten him up for a fight. With the rooster's victory, he hopes to change his fate. To physical misery—his old age, his hunger, his constipation—García Márquez opposed his spiritual grandeur. Classically structured, the language is concise, sober, dominated by a preoccupation with efficacy taken from journalism. Bare-bones realism predominates: like his character, the author awaited a letter with money, which never arrived, and also didn't know whether he would eat on the next day.

The last boat to come in was the mail boat. The colonel watched it dock, dull with anxiety. On the roof, tied to the smokestacks and protected by an oilskin, he discerned the mailbag. Fifteen years of waiting had sharpened his intuition. The rooster had sharpened his anxiety.

At the post office, the clerk delivers a package of periodicals and mail to the doctor, and says the usual 'Nothing for the colonel'. 'I wasn't expecting anything. There's no one to write to me,' lies the colonel.

The doctor, a liaison for the guerrillas, visits the colonel's house to examine his wife, who is recovering from an asthma attack. He gives the colonel an envelope with 'what yesterday's papers didn't carry'.

It was a summary of the most recent national events, mimeographed for circulation through the underground. Revelations about the state of armed resistance in the interior of the country. He felt defeated.

'Circulate it,' the doctor told him.

The colonel goes to the tailor's shop to take the letter to Agustin's companions, 'it was his last refuge after his compatriots had been killed or exiled from the town and he had come a man alone...'

His wife works miracles to sustain the household economy. The colonel visits his lawyer to claim the documents accrediting him as treasurer of the revolution in Macondo, especially a valuable receipt, hand-written by Colonel Aureliano Buendía, chief of the rebel forces. After listening to an explanation of the bureaucratic tangle, the lawyer says…

In the house, there is nothing left to eat, but the colonel doesn't lose his sense of humour. Only hope of the letter sustains him.

The colonel visits the friends of Agustin, whose name serves as a password for the guerrillas in the hills. He offers them the rooster so that they will take on the job of feeding it. But instead of accepting the gift, they give him food for the rooster.

Weeks later, while the colonel and his wife are eating a plate of corn soup in the kitchen, the rooster, tied to the stove, peers at them suspiciously.

It's really good, where did you get it?

From the rooster.

The boys have brought it so much corn that it decided to share it with us. Such is life.

Life is the best thing that has been invented. This is a money-spinning rooster, it will feed us for three years.

You can't eat dreams.

You don't eat them, but they sustain you.

Furniture, ornaments, even the wedding rings have all gone from the house. The entire town is involved with the rooster. The colonel fights on to the end. His wife, the voice of common sense, confronts the colonel, whose character is the opposite.

If the rooster wins. But if it loses? Haven't you thought that it could lose?

...and meanwhile, what will we eat?

It can't lose. We've still got forty days to make sure of it.

Shit.

With the colonel, García Márquez rounded off a powerful metaphor. He re-wrote the novel nine times—superstition?—until he finished this small work of art in January 1957. Meanwhile, Plinio Mendoza had gone to Caracas to work for two magazines, *Elite* and *Momento*. Gabo didn't have a bad time of it. He had a dozen bohemian friends—Latin Americans, Arabs, Frenchmen—to hang out with.

Toward the end of 1956 he moved to a *chambre de bonne*, where he had a romance with **Tachia Quintana**, a generous and 'reckless Basque'. This brief and tempestuous love affair made it possible for him to continue writing. In Tachia's room, Gabo wrote furiously on the typewriter, smoking incessantly.

As a couple they had no future, but it was the beginning of a beautiful friendship.

One day his path crossed that of **Ernest Hemingway** on the Boulevard St. Michel, but his shyness stopped him from approaching. On another day, after Plinio Mendoza had returned, the friends were travelling through East and West Germany, Russia and the Ukraine with the idea of seeing 'real Socialism' in action. Two years before, García Márquez had travelled to Poland and Czechoslovakia as a correspondent for *El Espectador*.

Getting a visa for the Soviet Union, other than for an official visit, was at the time virtually impossible. Back in Paris, an opportunity presented itself. Manuel Zapata Olivella's 'Delia Zapata', the Colombian folklore group had just arrived in Paris, invited to the VIth Youth Congress in Moscow. Since a saxophonist and an accordionist were missing, Gabriel and Plinio got their visas as counterfeit members of the group.

His trip through the Socialist countries is documented in articles published in *Elite* in Caracas and *Cromos* in Bogotá in 1959. Twenty years later a pirated edition (eventually authorised and called ***90 Days Behind the Iron Curtain***) gathered them together. The central idea was that in the so-called popular democracies there could be no authentic socialism because the prevailing system was not based on the native conditions of each individual country but was 'a system imposed from outside by the USSR through local communist parties that are dogmatic and lack imagination!'

In East Germany, everything looked ugly, uniform and grey. Despite the good and cheap food, the people were 'the glummest I have ever seen.'

Arriving in Czechoslovakia, he breathed easier in what seemed a less oppressive atmosphere. The Czechs looked happier.

It is the only Socialist country where people do not appear to suffer any nervous tension and where one does not have the impression—false or true—of being controlled by the secret police.

The USSR made him feel crushed, with its immense mosaic of peoples, languages, landscapes and human types.

...the dramatic contrasts of a country where the workers live crowded in one room and have the right to buy only two sets of clothing a year, while they gain weight on the satisfaction of knowing that a Soviet rocket has reached the moon...

His Soviet articles were indicative of a measure of political disenchantment. In Moscow, **Joseph Stalin** and the fervour he still generated in people four years after his death impressed him. On seeing the embalmed body of the dictator in his Red Square mausoleum, García Márquez again felt fascinated by another creature who possessed supreme power. Stalin seemed to enjoy the life of power beyond death.

Here the first outline of the patriarch appeared; another ubiquitous, outsized and all-powerful dictator.

In his exquisite and omnipotent cadaver, there was no remorse. His moustache and features exhaled a sort of timelessness, identical to that of his official portraits.

In November he travelled to London with the idea of studying English, doing some reporting and continuing work on the 'lampoons' novel. Shortly after his arrival, he received a telegram from Venezuela with a tempting offer.

YOU HAVE STAFF WRITER'S JOB IN MOMENTOS MAGAZINE STOP SENDING AIR TICKET IF YOU AGREE STOP REGARDS SIGNED PLINIO MENDOZA

Time to go back, said his intuition, the guide to all his vital decisions. Just before Christmas, 1957, he arrived in Caracas like someone answering a call of destiny. He was no stranger to Bolívar's birthplace. In Aracataca, he had heard the fairy tales told by Juana de Freites—the providential midwife—set in the fabulous Caracas of her memories.

When Plinio Mendoza introduced them...

On 1 January 1958, his first day off, when Plinio called for him, Gabo remarked:

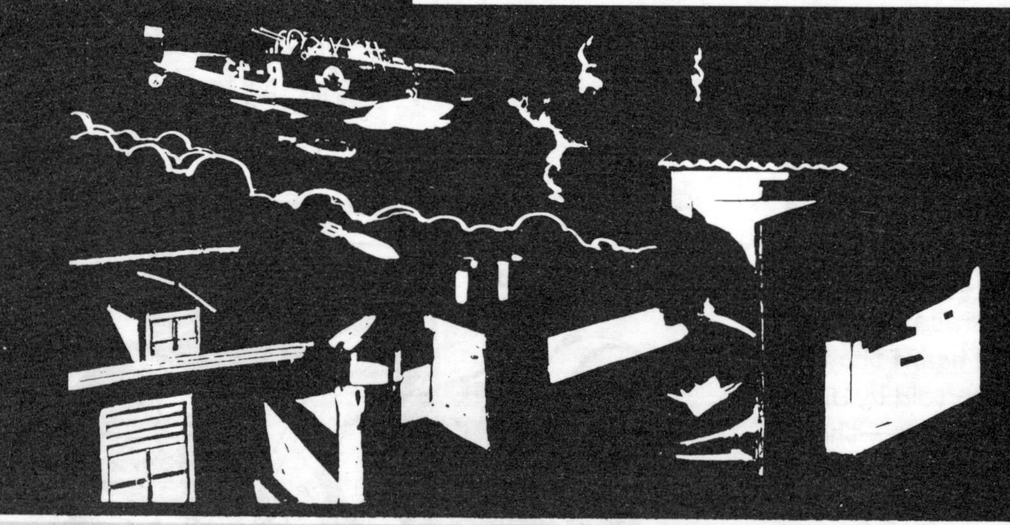

Minutes later, the bombardment of Miraflores, the presidential palace, began. Maracay Airforce Base rebelled in the first bid to oust the dictator **Marcos Pérez Jiménez**, who had been in power for six years.

In Plinio's flat, the sleepless friends listened to the radio, while through the picture window behind the balcony, shone the lights of a night-flying aircraft, gaining altitude as it headed out to sea.

The streetlights came on. People shouted, sang, waved flags from cars and trucks, embraced. Car horns, yells, factory sirens. The entire city erupted in delirium.

Three days later, in the president's anteroom the press awaited news of the formation of the governing junta, which was being discussed behind closed doors.

The sight of the officer sparked the idea of writing ***The Autumn of the Patriarch***. During those days, he talked with the presidential palace's major-domo, who had fifty years of service, dating from the bygone days of the Dictator **Juan Vicente Gómez**. The old general, who governed with an iron fist for thirty years, was the principal model for the Patriarch. Once again, the perception of the solitude of power came back to him from his childhood in Aracataca, from the legend of Grandfather Nicolás, the war veterans and the exiled Venezuelans, Generals **José Rosario Duran** and **Marcos Freites**. From exile, the dictator Gómez had become a figure of mythology. Obsessively, García Márquez started to amass documents on Latin American dictators.

In March 1958, he flew to Barranquilla to marry Mercedes. He told her of his plan to write a novel on the Latin American dictator and to finish *La Casa*.

And he made a third confession:

Mercedes didn't doubt that it would be so. She also knew that her contribution would be vital if he were to achieve his goal. In the San Bernardino flat, Gabo wrote the stories for *Big Mama's Funeral*, which ended up at the bottom of a suitcase.

The visit of U.S. Vice-President **Richard Nixon** led to his leaving *Momentos*, which had become the most popular magazine in Caracas. The people had not forgotten that the U.S. President, Dwight Eisenhower, had decorated the deposed dictator.

The editor of the magazine wrote a public letter of apology to the U.S. government. As a sign of their disagreement, Plinio and Gabo published a rebuttal bearing the author's initials. The scandal ended with both of them resigning.

García Márquez went to work as city editor for the Venezuelan gossip magazine *Venezuela Gráfica*. But at the end of 1958, something happened in Latin America that changed his professional attitude and the destiny of his life: **the Cuban revolution**. Fulgencio Batista's dictatorship came tumbling down in the last days of December.

The victory of the 26 July Movement, headed by Fidel Castro, launched a new era in the region's history that generated a spirit of solidarity through the entire continent.

A few days later a representative of the 26 July Movement arrived in the newsroom to invite the journalists to Cuba to report on the progress of the 'truth operation' Fidel Castro was organising. The idea was to counteract the hostile press campaign orchestrated by the American agencies after the executions on the island.

Listen, Gabo, there's a plane to take you to Cuba to see the trial of Sosa Blanco, one of Batista's worst henchmen.

The impact was stark and painful, once he perceived the terror of a man who knew he was as good as dead.

When Plinio and Gabo arrived, they found that Havana was one big party. The Cubans were out in the streets, celebrating the advent of freedom.

García Márquez returned to Caracas imbued with the heroic and messianic atmosphere that Cuba was living. He wanted to translate his support into something practical. At that point, Plinio Mendoza returned to Colombia, and Gabo dreamed of going off to Mexico to make films and continue writing. But first...

At the beginning of 1959, because of the international press's constant disinformation regarding news about Cuba, the revolutionary government created the first Latin American press agency, **Prensa Latina**. An Argentinian journalist and a friend of Che Guevara, **Ricardo Masetti,** was the director. He came to Colombia to meet the new correspondents for Prensa Latina.

This was a happy period. For the first time, Gabo had a job that was independent of the capitalist centres of opinion, that coincided with his political ideas and also provided a good salary and a decent place to live. The agency became a Mecca for the Colombian Left. The future ministers, ambassadors and guerrilla chiefs of the seventies all paraded through there. In these offices, the youth movement of the **Movimiento Revolucionario Liberal** (MRL) was organised. Volunteers were also recruited to overthrow Leonidas Trujillo, the Dominican Republic's dictator.

Happiness was completed by the arrival of the García Márquez's first son, Rodrigo, on 24 August 1959. Plinio was his godfather and he was baptised by Camilo Torres, the friend of young people who was by then the priest of the poor and dispossessed. Camilo later died in the mountains fighting with the guerrillas of the **Ejército de Liberación Nacional** (National Liberation Army).

Recognition still failed to arrive. In 1959 the magazine Mitos published *No One Writes to the Colonel* (unauthorised and with no royalties), while the story 'Tuesday Siesta' (for many, his best) appeared in *El Heraldo* with an illustration by the Colombian artist **Fernando Botero**. The second revised edition of *Leaf Storm* was also published. His intense activity at Prensa Latina did not keep him from literature. In the Andean air of Bogotá, he worked on a new version of *In Evil Hour*. After a critical reading of the originals and a silent work of mental carpentry, Gabriel took the drastic decision to tear up the 500 pages and to start the book again from scratch.

So as not to let the story get out of hand, he established a rigorous schedule, with one chapter to be written every day. He delineated the space for each character, purged adjectives, avoided Faulkner, followed Hemingway. In three months, the novel he had started four years earlier was finished.

His friends couldn't understand why he put the novel away again.

The huge book would still travel through several countries in his suitcase, next to an awful jacket with electric stripes that Gabriel took everywhere.

Invited to Barranquilla to discuss the creation of a national federation of cinema clubs, García Márquez met the publisher **Alberto Aguirre**.

The book was published the following year and Gabo's prediction came true: out of two thousand copies, only eight hundred were sold.

In September 1960, he was asked by Masetti to open a new affiliate of Prensa Latina in New York.

PL had an impressive team of Latin American journalists who managed to raise the hackles of the U.S. media monopolies. One night at the airport, the Argentinian **Rudolfo Walsh**, Prensa Latina's Chief of Special Services in Havana, conducted the shortest interview of his life with Ernest Hemingway.

In Cuba, García Márquez spent three months tied to the teleprinter. At the time, nobody slept much. A U.S. invasion was expected at any moment and the city had been turned into one huge barricade. He spent almost all his time at the office, where everyone worked at an infernal pace. He shared an apartment with **Aroldo Wall**. The indefatigable Masetti was full of cryptic humour and was also imaginative, and as antagonistic to the Soviet-style Communist bureaucracy as Che. Gabo overcame Walsh's reserve and their talks about narrative structures became their best form of relaxation. Sometimes, at daybreak, there was time to just hang out.

Thanks to Masetti's nose for news, PL pinpointed—months before anyone else—the location of the hacienda Retaljuleu in Guatemala where the CIA was preparing the invasion of Cuba. While checking news stories, a chaotic sequence of paragraphs in an All American Cable dispatch had caught his attention.

Walsh managed to decipher all of it with the aid of a cryptographer's manual. It turned out to be a report to Washington carrying the details of the armed landing on Playa Giron in April 1961. Gabo was invited to share in this supreme moment for a journalist.

Gabo went to meet **Felix Caignet**, the celebrated scriptwriter of the radio soaps he had listened to as a youngster. One day Gabo showed him the enormous manuscript for *La Casa*, which had already been the source of four books. The old master explained to him that texts had to read well and sound right, in the tradition of oral literature. He gave him a couple of tips, which were, for him, the two great secrets of the art of storytelling:

Something always has to happen in every paragraph because people like to be told stories, and dislike description or disquisition.

A changed order of words that may appear to work as 'literature' often does not carry a narrative line well, and if every paragraph has uncomfortable phrases, readers will feel like skipping them. Best to keep to the natural order of grammar so the text flows.

García Márquez arrived in New York with Mercedes and Rodrigo early in 1961, the year of 'sectarianism' in Cuba. A group of old Communists headed by **Anibal Escalante** was hogging government posts, and PL was one of their targets. Masetti resisted, but certain correspondents received threats from the exiles.

At night he corrected and polished *In Evil Hour*, and in the meantime the anti-Castro campaign escalated into hysteria. Soon after, the U.S. invasion of Cuba took place. In a week, the populace was celebrating 'the first defeat of Imperialism in the American Hemisphere'. Masetti left PL and enlisted as a soldier in the rebel army. Plinio Mendoza and García Márquez resigned in solidarity with Masetti. Penniless once again, Gabo decided to go to Mexico. But first, he wanted to have a look at the American South of Faulkner, his mentor.

This involved twenty days of infernal travel over burning hot and dismal back roads...

With twenty dollars in his pocket, he landed in Mexico on the very day that Hemingway ended his life. His friend Alvaro Mutis helped him to find a place to live. On the following day...

That night he wrote a moving homage, 'A Man Has Died a Natural Death'.

> Time will prove that Hemingway, a minor writer, will outshine many great writers because of his understanding of the motivations of men, and of the secrets of his craft... His transcendence is founded on an occult knowledge that keeps afloat an objective work, with a direct and simple structure, bare sometimes even in its drama.

Reading the Mexican novelist **Juan Rulfo**'s books was like a thunderbolt. As previously with Kafka, Melville, Sophocles, Faulkner and Woolf, García Márquez became an ardent admirer of Rulfo. Under this influence, he wrote 'The Sea of Lost Time', an allegoric and fantasy-filled tale, the prelude to *One Hundred Years of Solitude*. But four years would elapse before he sat down to write that particular novel.

In Mexico he wanted to work as a scriptwriter, have an editorial platform for the Americas, and write. He found no work in films, though, and went back to frivolous journalism, editing two women's magazines on condition that his name would not appear in them.

On 16 April 1962, *Gonzalo*, his second son, was born, bringing good luck with him. *In Evil Hour* won the national prize for fiction sponsored by Esso (a three-thousand-dollar award) and *Big Mama's Funeral* brought in a thousand Mexican pesos in royalties—the first moment of plenty in his life.

With Mutis, he went to work at an advertising agency. Then he began to write new-wave film scripts with the writer **Carlos Fuentes,** who 'translated' the Colombian's dialogues into Mexican. In 1964—his golden year in cinema—he wrote ***Time to Die***, his first original script. The following year, **Arturo Ripstein** directed the film—a Mexican cowboy and Indian saga.

Time to Die revealed that García Márquez was trying to communicate in films the same obsessions he had in literature. Revenge, honour and tragic destiny are the themes that drive the action. Both time and the structure of the story are circular and reiterative; the characters and situations 'Macondian'. It all carries the seal of García Márquez's literary reality.

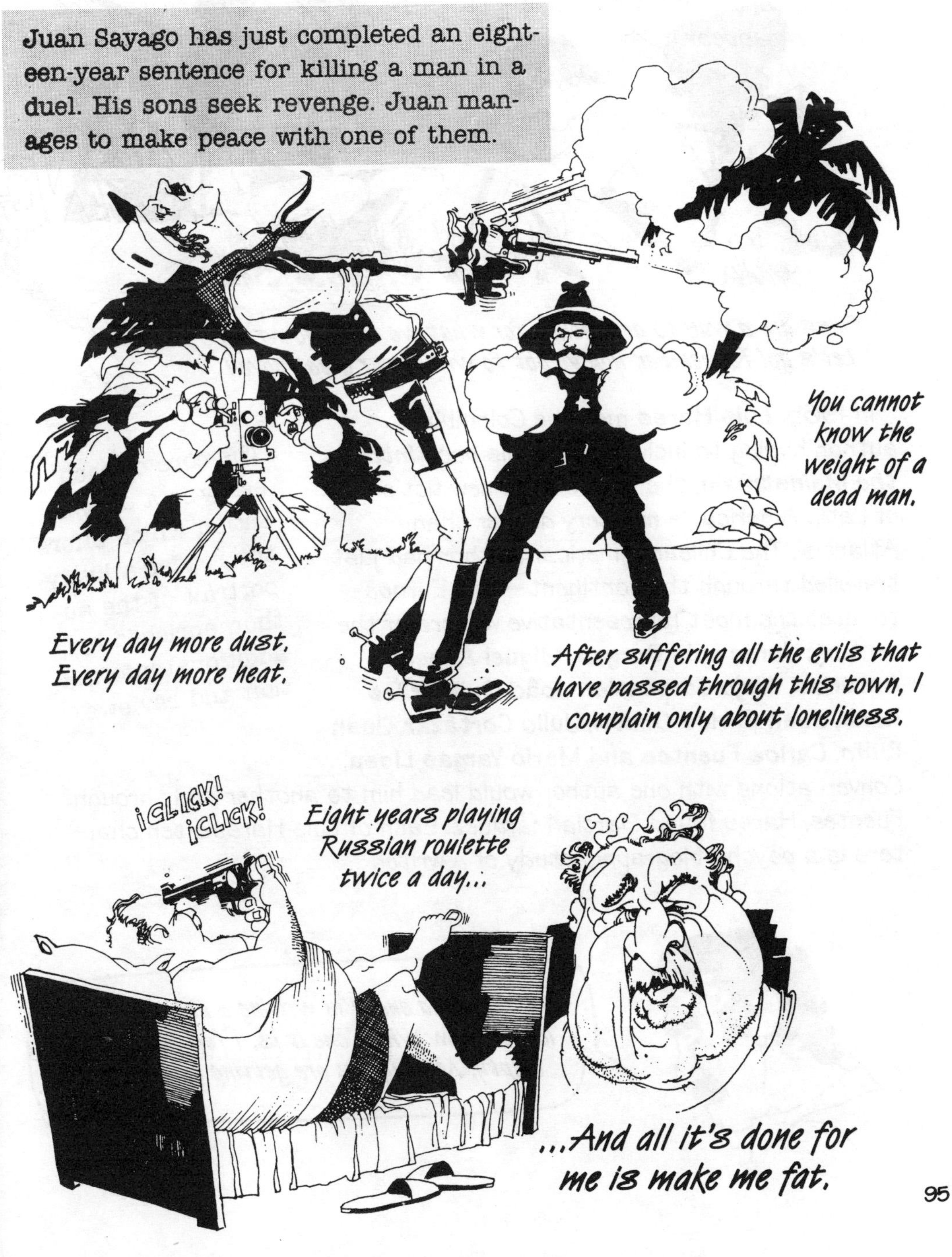

Juan Sayago has just completed an eighteen-year sentence for killing a man in a duel. His sons seek revenge. Juan manages to make peace with one of them.

You cannot know the weight of a dead man.

Every day more dust. Every day more heat.

After suffering all the evils that have passed through this town, I complain only about loneliness.

After several failures, García Márquez realized that films were not the perfect means of expression he had thought they were. At that point, Gabo and Carlos Fuentes were regretting their failures in film and consoling one other.

In 1965, **Luis Harss** met the Colombian author, hoping to include him in his book ***Into the Mainstream***, the first on the new fiction of Latin America, 'a mystery deeper than Atlantis'. The Chilean-American author had just travelled through the continent—and Europe—to meet the most representative writers of the century: **Jorge Luis Borges, Miguel Angel Asturias, Alejo Carpentier, Joâo Guimarâes Rosa, Juan Carlos Onetti, Julio Cortázar, Juan Rulfo, Carlos Fuentes** and **Mario Vargas Llosa**. Conversations with one author would lead him to another and through Fuentes, Harss found García Márquez. Each of Luis Harss's ten chapters is a psycho-biographic study of a writer.

> The core of each essay is a conversation which offers the reader a lively portrait of the author, enriched by additional information and reviews

One day, on the way to Acapulco with his family, he was struck by a revelation: he must complete, the novel that he had been writing since he was twenty. All of a sudden, he knew how to write it.

I've found the voice! I'm going to tell the story poker-faced, just like my grandmother did with her fantastic stories, and starting from the afternoon when the boy is taken by his father to discover ice.

With his savings and Mutis' help, he scraped together five thousand dollars so that Mercedes could manage the house while he shut himself away to write the novel.

One Hundred Years of Solitude

García Márquez shut himself away for eighteen months in the 'Cave of the Mafia', his studio-bunker at the back of the house. From eight o'clock in the morning until three in the afternoon he wrote ***One Hundred Years of Solitude***, and then spent the evening doing research and preparing the following day's work. His mania for documentation led him to consult alchemy texts, seafarers' tales, the chronicles of medieval plagues, manuals of poisons and antidotes, the histories of Latin America, treatises on civil wars and ancient arms, studies of scurvy, beriberi and pellagra, as well as the Encyclopaedia Britannica and sundry dictionaries. He was now going to give literary expression to the early experiences that had made such a deep impression on him.

I wished to leave a poetical record of the world of my childhood, which had been passed, with some sadness, in a large house, with a sister who ate earth, a grandmother who divined the future, and numerous relatives with the same name who never made much of a distinction between happiness and madness.

He perfected that famous first sentence which opens his masterpiece...

Many years later, facing the firing squad, Colonel Aureliano Buendía would remember that distant afternoon when his father took him to discover ice.

He wrote that he 'needed the ice in that first sentence because in a town that is the hottest in the world, ice is the most marvellous thing. If it hadn't been hot, the book would never have existed. It was unnecessary to remark on the intensity of the heat again; it was in the air.'

At night, friends would troop by to hang out and talk about the work in progress.

In November 1965, García Márquez wrote a letter to Luis Harss telling him about *One Hundred Years of Solitude*, for inclusion in Harss's book.

It is, in a way, my first novel that I began writing at 17, but now I've enlarged its scope. It is not just Colonel Aureliano Buendía's story but the story of his entire family, from the foundation of Macondo up to when the last Buendía commits suicide one hundred years later, and the line is extinguished.

It will be like the framework for a puzzle whose pieces I have been providing in preceding books. All the keys are here. We see the origin and end of the characters, and the complete story of Macondo with no elisions.

Though in this novel carpets fly, the dead rise and flowers rain down, it is perhaps the least mysterious of all my books, because the author tries to lead the reader by the hand so that he should not get lost at any moment, nor any point remain obscure. I am ending my Macondo cycle with this book and there'll be a complete change of topic in the future.

In Buenos Aires, Harss presented the manuscript for his book *Into the Mainstream* to **Francisco Porrua**, the literary editor of Editorial Sudamericana.

The only writer that Porrua had not heard of was García Márquez. Besides telling him who García Márquez was and where he lived, Harss loaned him his four books. Porrua liked them a lot and wrote to García Márquez, offering to republish them. The author sent him a fragment of his latest novel and received a contract and a $500 advance by return of post. During a quick trip to Colombia for the première of *Time to Die*, he gave the first chapters to his Barranquilla friends. He also sent them to his friend Carlos Fuentes, who was in Paris. Fuentes was fascinated and wrote an article, which was published in Mexico in the literary supplement of *Siempre!*

From newspaper stories and advance extracts of the novel in a number of magazines—including *El Espectador* in Bogotá—a great rush of enthusiasm and expectation swept through the continent in advance of publication.

In *One Hundred Years of Solitude* family names (and destinies) are often repeated according to Macondo custom and Latin American tradition, sometimes leading to confusion.

It was the custom of the Buendías to name sons after their fathers. In order to distinguish between them, it is useful to remember that the José Arcadios continue the line, but the Aurelianos do not—with the sole exception of José Arcadio Segundo and Aureliano Segundo who, as they were identical twins, were confused in infancy.

GENEALOGY OF THE BUENDÍAS

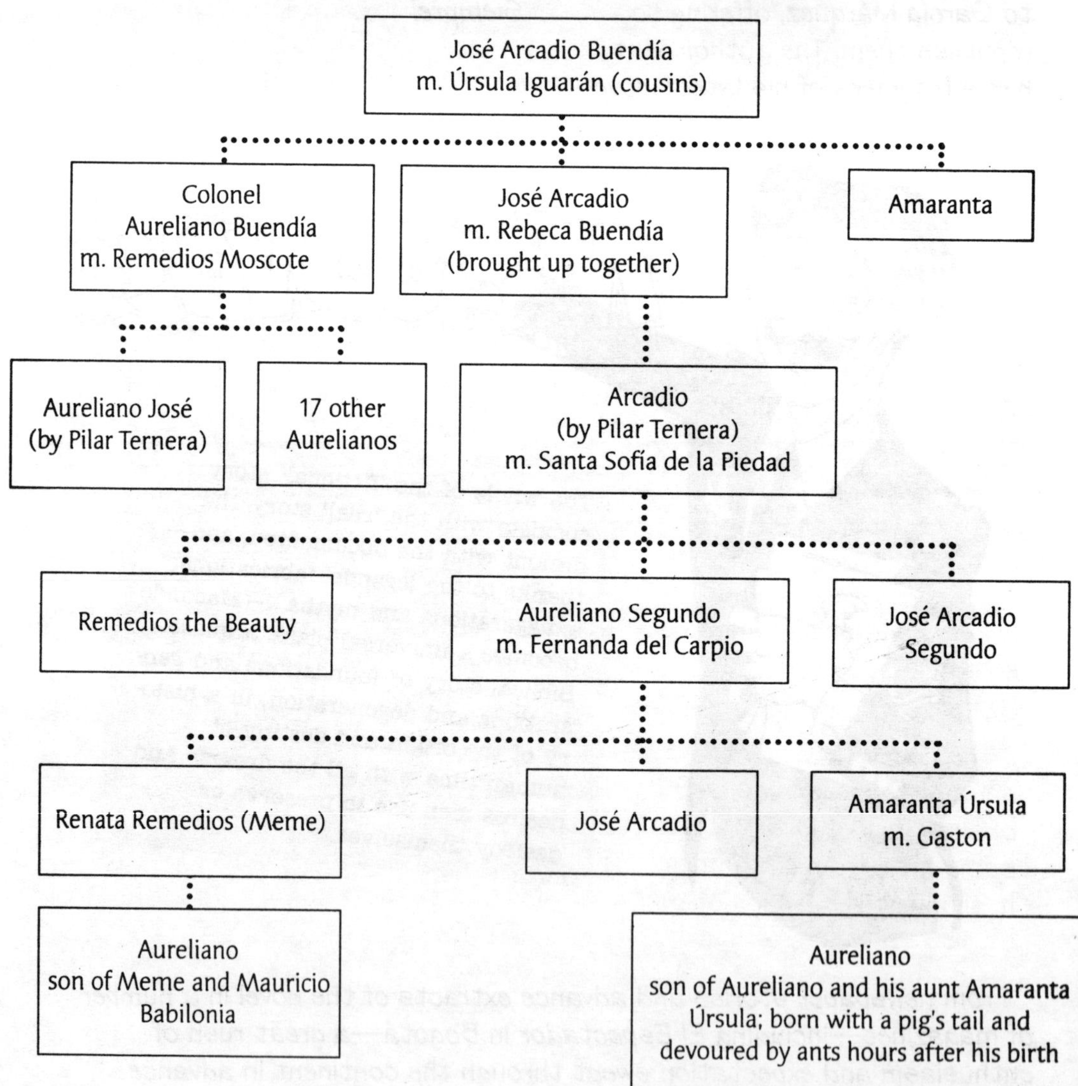

With *One Hundred Years of Solitude*, García Márquez allowed his imagination to take flight. The Earth could be round like an orange; a woman could ascend to heaven body and soul; and circus gypsies could bring the latest advances in science.

All the time that I was writing my previous books, I felt that something was missing, but I didn't know what. I only knew that I wanted to create a fresco of generations of one family in which everything would happen.

He left no loose ends. All his previous paths came together in *One Hundred Years of Solitude*: characters, settings, scenes, situations, gestures and phrases, all melded into a complete literary reality. In *The Rebel*, Albert Camus (whom he greatly admires), writes:

The aim of great literature consists of creating a closed universe, or a perfect type... The fictional world is nothing but a correction of this world we live in.... [The novelist] aims to unity and thus reveals a metaphysical need.

The history of the mythical Macondo is told through the saga of the Buendías, a tribe condemned to solitude because of their lack of love. Both the town and the family share the same fate, from birth up to the final ruin when the wind sweeps it all away. The action opens in Macondo...

A village of twenty mud-and-wattle huts built on the banks of a river of crystal clear water rushing over a bed of stones—polished, white and enormous like prehistoric eggs. The world was so recent that many things lacked a name, and to refer to them one had to point them out with a finger.

Every year during May, a family of ragged gypsies set up their tents near to the village and with much to-do, showed their new inventions.

They are the tribe of the visionary Melquíades, a globe-trotting magus and expert in esoteric and obscure knowledge. In successive transformations he has survived all the plagues of the universe. This gypsy, a key character in the book, befriends José Arcadio Buendía who is Macondo's young patriarch and a rare mix of entrepreneur, quasi-scientist and mad inventor.

In search of a route that would put Macondo in touch with the great inventions, José Arcadio Buendía organises an expedition which takes them to the middle of the jungle, where they discover a Spanish galleon.

The entire structure seemed to occupy its own space of solitude and oblivion, sheltered from the ravages of time.

In the chronicle there is an abundance of surrealist scenes. Everyday life is invaded by the extraordinary as if they are natural occurrences. García Márquez drew his inspiration from real experiences, but he enriched them with exaggeration and fantasy.

When the gypsies next return to Macondo, it is with news of the death of Melquíades who had 'succumbed to fever on the beach at Singapore'. The chapter closes with the encounter with ice, that is anticipated in the first sentence of the book. This device of presenting and linking episodes like circles in a closed universe, is repeated throughout the novel.

...an enormous transparent block, with infinite internal needles where the light of sunset was shattered into coloured stars.

José Arcadio Buendía and his wife Úrsula have come to Macondo from Riohacha, hoping to start a new life. They are cousins and have married despite the predictions that they would have a son with a pig's tail. Úrsula is so frightened that she refuses to consummate the marriage. However, the gossip spreads that the reason she is still a virgin, is that her husband is impotent. One day, when José Arcadio wins a cockfight against Prudencio Aguilar...

That night, in a duel of honour José Arcadio Buendía fatally pierces Prudencio Aguilar's throat with a spear...

But José Arcadio Buendía and Úrsula are tormented by the look of utter desolation on the face of the corpse and so they set out across the sierra and found the village of Macondo where their three sons will grow up. One of them, Colonel Aureliano Buendía, is the outstanding member of the second generation. Many tales of wonder and adventure are told about him

Colonel Aureliano Buendía instigated thirty-two uprisings, all of which he lost. He fathered seventeen male children by seventeen different women and they were all exterminated in a single night... He survived fourteen attempts on his life, seventy-three ambushes and a firing squad.

He managed to become the Commander-in-Chief of the revolutionary forces... and the man most feared by the government, but he never allowed anyone to take his photograph. He declined the lifetime pension offered to him after the war and survived to old age on the small gold fish he made in his workshop in Macondo.

Nearly all my characters are like puzzles assembled from pieces of many different people and, certainly, including pieces of myself.

The image of his grandfather Nicolás Márquez is projected on to the entire line. Although Colonel Buendía is described as resembling General Uribe in appearance, he is also depicted as an accomplished goldsmith and a great fornicator and, like Nicolás, his war adventures establish the Buendías' social position in Macondo. Through the character of Úrsula we are given another clue to distinguishing the two male lines.

While the Aurelianos were withdrawn, but with lucid minds, the José Arcadios were impulsive and enterprising, but marked by a tragic destiny.

José Arcadio Buendía becomes insane in old age and dies tied to a chestnut tree. The colonel, endowed with the author's talent for premonition, had warned Úrsula two weeks earlier: 'Take good care of Papa because he is going to die.'

So many flowers fell from heaven that, at daybreak, the streets were carpeted with a compact layer that had to be cleared away with shovels and rakes to allow the funeral procession to pass by.

The death of José Arcadio the son is 'perhaps the only mystery that was never cleared up in Macondo.' After the fatal shot, a rivulet of blood flowed from his body and threaded a course through Macondo to where his mother was.

The slightly built, energetic and magnificent Úrsula is another central character in the book. While the men are busy with their crazy schemes and fighting and drinking, she embodies the characteristics of the earth mother, holding the world together.

This is the secret of the extraordinary longevity of this woman who guides that house of madmen through all their hazardous enterprises. The house, full of ghosts (living and dead), also mirrors the changing fortunes in the life of the town: waves of immigrants, plagues of insomnia, the banana fever, progress, decadence. Blind and half-mad, Úrsula only becomes resigned to dying after the flood that coincides with the banana company's departure, after the massacre of the workers.

Despite the fear of siring monsters, Buendían men cannot resist dicing with danger in their sexual relationships with family members. José Arcadio and Colonel Aureliano Buendía are irretrievably attracted to the 'scent of smoke' of the mature Pilar Ternera, with whom each makes love and fathers a son. José Arcadio marries Rebeca Buendía, with whom he grew up while Colonel Aureliano Buendía marries Remedios Moscote, a thirteen-year-old who could have been his daughter. Aureliano José and his aunt Amaranta have a clandestine and passionate affair, with no ill consequences. Amaranta's great-great-grandson, the seminarian José Arcadio also has dreams and fantasies about her until his death (drowned in the bathtub).

The novel can be read in an infinite number of ways. Certainly, there are many books, articles, essays and critical appraisals of it but, above all, this is a magical book, to be enjoyed. It is filled with memorable characters, luminous and lovely prose. Everything in it has the aura of vitality. Just as the 'magic' reveals a way of looking at the reality of Latin America, the humour prevents one from committing the (grave) error of taking seriously what is pure leg-pulling. As a good Caribbean, Gabo enjoyed telling stories with a poker-face just as his grandmother Tranquilina did.

In that forgotten Macondo... where the dust and heat had become so tenacious that it was hard to breathe, secluded by solitude and love and by the solitude of love in a house where it was nearly impossible to sleep because of the noise of the ants, Aureliano and Amaranta Úrsula were the only happy beings, and the happiest on earth.

Amaranta Úrsula, the emancipated version of Úrsula, dies giving birth to the son with a pig's tail, the only one of the line who had been conceived with love. Distraught, Aureliano wanders through the deserted streets of the town. He returns to the house to find that his son is also dead.

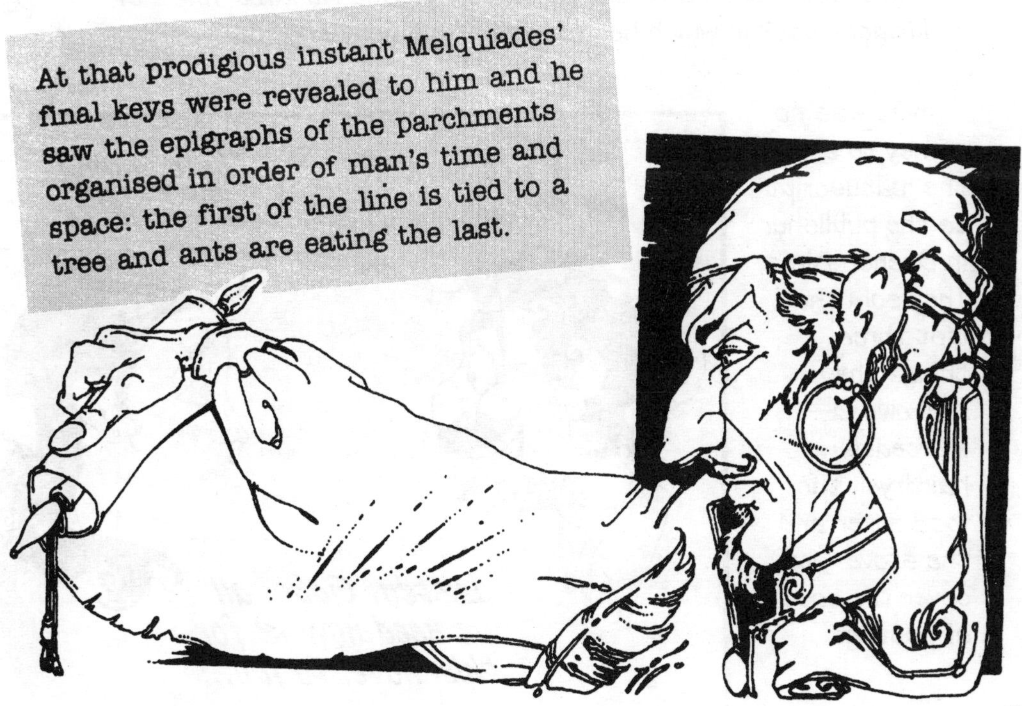

The readers and Aureliano together discover that Melquíades had written the story of Macondo and the family one hundred years previously. In Sanskrit and coded verse, he had concentrated a century of everyday episodes so as to make them coexist in a moment of time. Finally, it is clear that the manuscripts, adapted into novel form, are the novel itself: Melquíades is the narrator of *One Hundred Years of Solitude.* In this way, García Márquez closed the circle of his literary reality. The world had run its course.

Before reaching the final verse he had already understood that he would never leave that room, for it was written that the city of mirrors (or illusions) would be laid waste by the wind and exiled from the memory of men at the moment that Aureliano Babilonia finished deciphering the parchments, and that everything written on them was unrepeatable from always and forever, for races condemned to one hundred years of solitude did not have a second chance on earth.

One morning in September, the book reached its natural end. Then Gabo learned that their household debt had amounted to ten thousand dollars. But Mercedes had taken care of everything. Without her, García Márquez would not have been able to write *One Hundred Years of Solitude,* a book in which he unfurled all his genius.

There was no money to send the manuscript to the publisher in Buenos Aires. They sold the last three things they still owned—Mercedes' hairdryer, the food mixer and the stove—to cover the cost of postage.

Buenos Aires Was A Fiesta

Paco Porrua knew that the book would become part of history. His friend **Tomas Eloy Martínez**, the news editor of *Primera Plana*, caught Porrua's enthusiasm and they agreed to invite García Márquez to Buenos Aires. Early on the morning of 20 June, García Márquez never imagined that the Argentinian edition of *One Hundred Years of Solitude* would change the course of his life.

Anonymity lasted no time at all. In that magical city of Borges and Cortázar, García Márquez became acquainted with fame.

The entire city succumbed to the novel immediately and set about reading it.

Barely a few days had passed before mayhem descended and he had to be moved from one hotel to another and given a secretary to filter phone calls.

This runaway success took everyone by surprise: 30,000 copies were sold in the first week. In just three years, 600,000 copies were sold in Spanish rising to two million in eight years. In a few months his literary agent negotiated contracts for eighteen translations. By 1998, the novel had sold over twenty million copies worldwide.

One night Gabriel and Mercedes attended the opening night of a play at the Instituto di Tella.

The entire theatre rose to its feet. At that precise moment, I saw fame descending from heaven, wrapped in a brilliance of sheets beating softly like wings—like for Remedios the Beauty—and casting over García Márquez one of those shafts of light that are immune to the ravages of time.

Time for Revenge

The publication of the novel meant that a long period of waiting had ended. For the first time, Gabo was able to devote himself to being a professional writer.

He was going to have to learn to live with the fame that descended on him. He had not expected it, and his new role as a celebrity bothered him. He thought of moving to Spain to write the novel of dictatorship, *The Autumn of the Patriarch*, '...in the same vein of reckless Latin American realism'. However, he went first to the 13th International Congress of Latin American Literature in Caracas. At the airport he met the Peruvian author, **Mario Vargas Llosa**. They had corresponded but had never met. Now that they did, they became friends.

As a break between novels, García Márquez wrote four short stories, 'A Very Old Man with Enormous Wings', 'The Handsomest Drowned Man in the World', 'Blacamán the Good, Vendor of Miracles' and 'The Last Voyage of the Phantom Ship', published in magazines between 1968 and 1971. He dropped the idea of writing a book of children's stories in order to write a film script, *The Incredible and Sad Tale of Innocent Eréndira and Her Heartless Grandmother*, published in story form in 1972. This is the tale of a fourteen-year-old girl who is forced into prostitution in order to pay for her grandmother's house, which a moment of inattention has caused to burn down.

The story describes the adventures of two women living in the desert. It is a hostile environment through which marginal and nomadic people, such as gypsies, Indians and smugglers wander. The old woman and the girl live in a tent erected on the outskirts of towns which doubles as a brothel. As the business flourishes, Eréndira's clients form lines a kilometre long. Finally, the girl's lover, Ulises, kills the girl's grandmother and ends the years of prostitution.

García Márquez was never interested in any idea which could not stand the test of time. In order to be able to write, he needed a clear, simple idea that time had not been able to destroy.

The image of a very old despot living alone in a palace filled with cows triggered the story of *The Autumn of the Patriarch*. He used the same technique as that used in *Leaf Storm*: the various points of view of the people standing around a corpse. The difference now was that García Márquez had developed enormous wings and had the freedom to fly as he wished. He no longer felt constricted by language, syntax, time, geography or history. The use of multiple monologues (different voices telling the same story in different ways) reflected life under a dictatorship.

In this novel, a number of unidentified voices speak, as happens in history and in those Caribbean conspiracies that are full of secrets that everyone knows. There is a also strong musical influence here.

While he wrote, he listened to his favourite composer, Béla Bartok, and to all the popular music of the Caribbean. The mix, of course, was explosive. His love of music was a closely-guarded secret. He didn't like to listen to music or speak about it, except with his closest friends.

Experience has taught me that of all music, the most moving and heartfelt is to be found in the sentimental boleros of the Caribbean. The intellectuals know it but are ashamed to admit it incase they are thought to be uncultured.

From the point of view of language, this is the most vernacular of his books, with many Caribbean expressions, sayings and songs. Translators have gone mad trying to make sense of phrases that any Barranquilla taxi driver would latch on to immediately. It is full of arcane references to Rubén Darío, who even makes a brief appearance, and whom he quotes:

There was a cipher in your white handkerchief, red cipher of a name which was not yours, owner of my heart.

The spiral structure of the book makes it possible to compress time and so include much more. There are many long paragraphs without full stops or semicolons, in which different narrative points of view are woven together.

He discarded two versions. A monologue by the dictator sentenced to death was dropped because it did not accord with history. Dictators died of old age, were killed or fled the country. They were not tried. Fictionalised biography can work, but he didn't want it to look like *One Hundred Years of Solitude*. To get the feel of it, he moved to Franco's Spain, where he saw what everyday life was like under an old-fashioned dictatorship. But he was unable to infuse enough heat into the city of the book; his dictator's country is a Caribbean one where it is searingly hot.

He spent close to a year of his life wandering about the Lesser Antilles, from island to island. When he returned, he planted a few things, added the scent of something, and—*voilà!*—created the illusion of heat. The book was finished without mishap. The result was a coastal Caribbean book, a flight of fancy which he permitted himself when he decided to write just as he wished. It was also a confessional book, a coded autobiography, filled with personal experiences.

When *The Autumn of the Patriarch* was published in 1975, many complained that it was a difficult book to read, that a certain literary initiation was needed.

It was also the book that took him the longest to write. Without the financial security that *One Hundred Years of Solitude* afforded him, he would have been unable to write it. In *The Autumn of the Patriarch*, García Márquez shows all the culture of the Caribbean, beginning with his own. We find the brothel in Barranquilla, ('Matilde Arenales' beds for hire'), the Cartagena of his student days, the bars in the port where he would eat after leaving the paper at four in the morning, and even the schooners that sailed to Aruba and Curaçao loaded with whores.

The first sentence of the book is of prime importance:

During the weekend the vultures got in through the balconies of the presidential house, pecking to bits the wire mesh of the windows and stirring with their wings the stagnant time inside, and at daybreak on Monday the city awoke from its centuries-old lethargy under the warm, soft breeze of an important corpse and rotting grandeur.

They find the Patriarch's body in his office. The death of the Patriarch has been witnessed before. At the beginning of his 'autumn' his double, Patricio Aragones, dies, wounded by a poisoned dart.

...it's best not to talk about that, general, because it's better to be castrated with a mallet than to go around throwing mothers down onto the ground... only you could think that to be love, because it's the only love you know.

The dead body of his double gives the Patriarch the opportunity to stage his own mock death.

Bells of jubilation begin to ring and the drumbeat of freedom to throb. The Patriarch sees the assault troops dragging the body off, destroying everything in their way.

The Patriarch leaves his hiding place and bursts into the cabinet room, where they are dividing up the booty left behind at his death.

After a panicked stampede, he remains alone with his crony, General Rodrigo de Aguilar, who warns him to get down, because 'the real fireworks' are about to begin.

On one 'historic October Friday' the Patriarch finds that everyone is **wear-ing** red birettas. The scene which confronts him, a mixture of two historical events—the arrival of Columbus and the landing of the Marines—did not respect the chronological time of their occurrence.

Some strangers have arrived, babbling in a peculiar dialect because they made 'the sea' feminine, not masculine. they called macaws parrots, canoes rafts, harpoons javelins... Trade grew, and soon after everybody was trading all of God's creations.

The Patriarch tries to understand the upheaval that is taking place before him.

In his research into despots, García Márquez found that the dictator Gómez had an imposing personality. He possessed such extraordinary intuition that it was more like the gift of divination. Like the Patriarch, he would announce his own death and then resurrect himself.

Gabo found that *Oedipus Rex*, his favourite book, had much to teach him. He also learned much from Plutarch, Suetonius and the biographers of Julius Caesar.

Gómez fascinated me so intensely that the Patriarch has much more of him than of the others.

Julius Caesar is the character I would have liked to create in literature.

The Patriarch was put together from the characteristics of many Latin American dictators, especially those from the Caribbean. Reading their biographies, he discovered that they were all deranged.

François 'Papa Doc' Duvalier of Haiti had all the black dogs in the country exterminated because he believed that one of his enemies had transmuted into a black dog to save himself from arrest or assassination.

General García Morena governed Ecuador for 16 years as an absolute monarch, and his funeral was conducted with his corpse dressed in full regalia, bemedalled and seated in the presidential chair.

Maximiliano Hernández Martínez of El Salvador had thirty thousand peasants killed. He also had every single street light in the country covered in red paper to combat a measles epidemic and he invented a pendulum to check for poison in food.

The dominant figure in the lives of history's most infamous despots is that of the mother. Their fathers do not appear to be significant. So, when the Patriarch's mother dies, he uses all the resources of his authority to have her canonised. Rather than just drawing a portrait of a feudal dictator, García Márquez was interested in the opportunity to reflect upon the mystery of individual power, its solitude and its misery. Power—the highest expression of ambition and will—is an overriding vocation: a passion that becomes a substitute for love. History shows that the powerful live under the whip of sexual frenzy.

The lieutenant of *In Evil Hour* was Gabo's first attempt to explore power at the modest level of a village mayor. The Patriarch was his most complex effort. The solitude of fame is like that of power and the strategy used to ward off fame is similar to that for holding on to power. In part, both fame and power are based on solitude. Lack of communication makes the problem worse and, eventually, information leads to isolation from an evasive and changing reality.

With power and fame comes the question: who to believe? Taken to its extremes, it gives rise to the ultimate question...

Who the hell am I?
Where the hell am I?

His status as a famous writer made García Márquez even more aware of this risk and helped him to create a patriarch who was no longer sure of his own name.

García Márquez acquired political capital: his reputation as a writer. He took advantage of his celebrity status to become an unofficial ambassador for Latin America. He intervened whenever he could in causes that mattered to him and that he defended. In the 1970s he became an activist in the defence of human rights and worked against American interference in the continent. He helped to found and support **Habeas**, an international human rights organisation.

He moved back to Mexico, travelling frequently to his other houses in Cartagena, Havana, Paris and Barcelona. He became friendly with progressive heads of government in Europe and Latin American. As a friend of Fidel Castro, Omar Torrijos Herrera of Panama, Carlos Andres Pérez of Venezuela, Alfonso Lopez Michelsen of Colombia and the Sandinistas in Nicaragua, he fitted easily into the role of unofficial intermediary around the Caribbean.

In my next incarnation, I want to be a writer…

His friendship with Castro was based on a sort of Caribbean complicity. Castro was a voracious reader and knowledgeable about the best literature. He showed Gabo an error of calculation in the speed of the ship *Aventura* in the *The Story of a Shipwrecked Sailor* and from then on Gabo let him read the manuscripts of his books.

In 1979, Gabo quite relished a little revenge. When Torrijos went to Washington to meet with President Jimmy Carter to sign the Panama Canal treaty, he added García Márquez and **Graham Greene** to his official party. Torrijos was determined to solve the problem of those intellectuals who were prohibited from entering the United States. As they descended from the official aircraft with their Panamanian passports, Gabo and Greene were secretly amused to listen to the resounding hymns and the booming cannons, in a welcome usually reserved for heads of state.

In 1981, François Mitterand, the French President, awarded Gabo the Legion of Honour and touched his heart by telling him: 'You belong to the world I love.'

When *Gabo* was in Colombia for the launch of *Chronicle of a Death Foretold*, in 1981, the Conservative government accused him of financing M-19, a guerrilla group. He sought political asylum in Mexico and left Bogotá in a flurry of scandal. In Cuba, the Argentinian writer **Osvaldo Soriano** wrote a piece for the satirical magazine, *Humor*:

He 'admits' that his career bears a certain resemblance to that of the exemplary Cassius Clay. What do people think of this champion who went headlong into politics, who earned millions and donated them to good causes? García Márquez doesn't compete or show off, but every one of his public gestures goes right around the world on the wires of the news services. Some compare his political asylum to Mohammed Ali's buffoonery in order to attract spectators. Are they equally gifted publicity hounds?

How does that power work? García Márquez says that he's just a simple, nice guy. But he knows that he can pick up a phone and, in five minutes, fix something that might take someone else a lifetime. At times, he wishes that he could press a button and make fame disappear. Sure, as long as he could use the same button to make it come back...

He hated having his life transformed into a spectacle. He has even felt a kind of resentment towards *One Hundred Years of Solitude*. 'It's as if it had got into my house to take over everything.'

Chronicle of a Death Foretold stands as the victory of a great narrator over his own legend. It is based on the real-life story of an atrocious crime in which a bride who is discovered not to be a virgin is returned to her family; to uphold the family honour, her two brothers kill the man they believe has dishonoured her. This was a common story in the fifties. García Márquez's tale is dominated by the image of Santiago Nasar, stabbed and held up by his assassins' daggers. The novel opens:

> **On the day they were going to kill him, Santiago Nasar got up at 5:30 in the morning to await the boat on which the bishop was arriving.**

The story is told with the precision of a surgeon.

This is arguably García Márquez's most complex novel. But will it last the two hundred years that he feels a 'good novel' needs in order to prove itself? He believes, with others, that the *Chronicle* is a great novel, but that, unlike *One Hundred Years of Solitude* it is not a memorable one. It is a writers' book.

In this novel you can see the nuts and bolts, like in a railroad carriage, as Hemingway said.

A writer reveals the keys to the text: the tip of the iceberg (Hemingway again) that allows an attentive reader to see through into the remaining four-fifths hidden under the precise, intricate writing that reminds you of a news report. The story has the meticulous structure of a detective novel.

I threw away thousands of sheets of paper to arrive at the final version of the Chronicle. This always happens. A fifteen-page story uses up 800 pages. A piece for a newspaper must be written several times. When a text goes downhill, I abandon it. It is useless to inject a dying man with serum.

Why did he wait so long to write this book? Well, his mother was upset at the idea that a book written by her son would contain so many people she knew, and even relatives. She asked him not to write the book while the victim's mother was still alive. But the subject had a major impact on him when he discovered one key fact: the two killers had not wanted to commit the crime and had done everything possible to get someone to stop them.

Although the real-life story ended nearly twenty-five years after the crime, when the husband returned to the wife he had repudiated, the book had to end with the detailed description of the crime. The solution was to introduce a narrator—for the first time, the author himself—who roves at will through the novel's layered time.

The best literary formula is always the truth.

As soon as the novel came out, journalists picked up the scent and went off to Sucre and published the real names of the participants. His mother pleaded with him, 'Son, I beg you to have that book withdrawn because it is doing such harm to a family we love very much.' Gabo replied, 'Mother, there are a million copies out on the streets.'

Chronicle of a Death Foretold was written a page a day. He began at nine and wrote until a page was ready, meaning that, in his judgment, it was perfect. He also used another technique learned from Hemingway: never let an idea exhaust itself at a single sitting; leave the page knowing how the story will continue, to make the following day's work easier. Ernest Hemingway's ghost wanders through the *Chronicle*, affecting its style; 'In the end, I always return to journalism, to the extreme economy of words.'

One morning in October 1982, he received a call from his friend Pierre Shori.

The Nobel Song and Dance

In December 1982, García Márquez arrived in Stockholm as the first snow of the year was falling. He was the fourth Latin American to receive the Nobel Prize for Literature. He stayed at the Grand Hotel with Mercedes and his son Gonzalo.

The first thing he did was to disappear from the hotel and to return holding a yellow rose, the emblem of Colombia and his personal talisman.

He took refuge in the country home of Olaf Palme, the newly-elected Socialist prime minister of Sweden, and a great friend.

When he received the prize from King Carl Gustav, Gabo chose as background music the *Intermezzo Interroto* from Bártok's *Concerto for Orchestra*.

Knowing that his speech would be widely broadcast, García Márquez laid out the life and culture of Latin America for his audience:

I dare to think that it is this outsized reality, and not only its literary expression, that has deserved the attention of the Swedish Academy of Letters. Poets and beggars, musicians and prophets, warriors and scoundrels, all creatures of that unbridled reality, we have had to ask but little of imagination, for our crucial problem has been a lack of conventional means to render our lives believable. This, my friends, is the crux of our solitude.

He then took the opportunity to ask for:

...a new and sweeping utopia of life, where no one will be able to decide for others how they die, where love will really prove true and happiness be possible; and where the races condemned to one hundred years of solitude will have at last and forever, a second opportunity on earth.

That night, his friends surprised him with a party and Colombian music. Sixty artists from his homeland were present. He celebrated by dancing the cumbia and the merengue.

The Newspaper That Never Was

He returned to Mexico, to his house in Pedregal, a neighbourhood of luxurious houses.

When I finished the Chronicle I felt that I was in a state of extreme solitude. I yearned for my years as a reporter, when I wasn't condemned to live with the disconcerting jolts of the imagination.

Tomás Eloy Martínez explained: 'A week after receiving the Nobel Prize, in order to find some peace of mind García Márquez conceived *El Otro*, a newspaper that was to die a premature death, "strangled by literature", seven months later'.

With the money from the prize and some private contributions, he embarked on the project with his characteristic obsessiveness. He put **Rodolfo Terragno**, a founder of *El Diario*, the Caracas newspaper, in charge of setting up the new paper, and asked Martínez to organise the newsroom. *El Otro* ('the other one') was the title of a story by Borges and at the same time suggested that García Márquez was also going to be a journalist on the paper. This complicated matters...

What kind of writing are people going to expect from a paper like this? Magical realism embellished with glittering adjectives, like The Autumn of the Patriarch? Or will it reproduce ad infinitum the latest political stories, written by the owner in fallow periods between one novel and the next?

There was hardly time to come up with an answer.

In June 1983, García Márquez began to share his doubts about the paper with Rodolfo Terragno.

Last night I couldn't sleep because the throbbing of the presses we're going to buy next month is driving me crazy.

I dreamed of a novel where an old man of 80 lives in a state of sexual frenzy with an old woman of 70. If I knew their names I'd be writing the story by now.

They set up a meeting. Although the staff of the newspaper were ready to start publishing, García Márquez wanted to shut himself away to write the novel about the two old people.

Do you want García Márquez's El Otro to come out without García Márquez being present.

That's exactly what I want.

Gabo, El Otro IS you. We can't step into your shoes.

So the newspaper staff refused to go ahead without him. Gabo tried to tell them what they already knew: that it is not possible to write a novel and a newspaper at the same time. He argued that although he was indispensable for the novel, they were all that was required for the paper. He couldn't delay writing the novel any longer because it was gnawing away at him. They told him the inevitable fate of the newspaper. He already knew.

Gabo continued to discuss the novel, until he found the perfect name for the old man in the story: Florentino Ariza. From then on, no one mentioned the paper again.

He settled into magical Cartagena de Indias, where his parents lived. It was their frustrated early courtship that inspired **Love in the Time of Cholera**. His father died before the novel was published in 1985. The story is set in 1870, in the countless nooks of the walled city. There the love story of Florentino Ariza and Fermina Daza is played out.

He woke up at five each morning, listened to the news and read until eight, when he sat down to begin work (on a computer now) until lunchtime. Then he would go down to the beach, where Mercedes awaited him with friends. The usual menu was freshly-caught fish, lobster or shrimp. In the evening, he visited his parents, questioning each of them separately. He'd wander around the streets, looking for places his characters would visit, chatting and soaking in the local dialect and atmosphere. In this way, on the next morning he would have new material, fresh off the street. In this novel, his fascination with plagues surfaced once again.

The city stood unchanging... the same burning, arid city of his nocturnal terrors and the solitary pleasures of puberty... where nothing had happened in four centuries, except for a slow aging amid the shrivelled laurels and rotting lagoons.

All of García Márquez's books touch and cross over each other. This need to tell the same story always, like a spiral, was born of nostalgia, the raw material at the heart of his writing. Not nostalgia for the 'good old days', but a way of looking at things from a particular vantage point. The story opens with a death.

Love in the Time of Cholera

It was inevitable that the scent of bitter almonds should always remind him of the fate of thwarted love. Dr. Juvenal Urbino sensed it immediately he entered the house, still in shadows, to which he had been called urgently to take care of a case that had ceased to be urgent many years before. The Antillean refugee, Jeremiah de Saint-Amour, a disabled war veteran, children's photographer and his most compassionate chess opponent, had placed himself beyond the torments of memory with the fumes of gold cyanide.

Born into medicine and fortune, Juvenal Urbino has gained prestige by conjuring a cholera epidemic into oblivion. He has been married to Fermina Daza for over fifty years. After discovering the real identity of his suicidal friend, he dies falling out of a mango tree when trying to catch a parrot.

Going back in time, we meet Florentino, the eighteen-year-old only son of a hard-working single mother. He is a telegraph operator's assistant, plays the violin and recites sentimental poetry. He is in love with Fermina.

Aunt Mama was the model for Aunt Escolastica, who in the novel watches over the love between Florentino and Fermina.

Would you please leave me alone for a moment with the senorita? I have something important to say to her.

How dare you! There's nothing you can say to her that I cannot hear.

Then I will not say anything to her. But I warn you, you will be responsible for the consequences.

After a feverish correspondence, Florentino proposes marriage. Fermina's father, a Spanish immigrant involved in shady business dealings, opposes the match.

Fermina's father takes her on a 'journey of forgetting'. But he makes the mistake of sending a telegraph to his brothers-in-law, announcing their arrival. Florentino, with the complicity of his fellow telegraph operators, is able to find out their complete itinerary, and to maintain intensive communication with Fermina for over a year.

Fermina eventually rejects Florentino and marries Doctor Urbino, the most sought-after bachelor, who has just returned from a long stay in Paris. In his despair, Florentino makes a trip up the Magdalena River that evokes the author's youth.

While Florentino stays single though not celibate, Fermina feels as if her life is on loan from her husband: 'she was the absolute sovereign of a vast empire of happiness built by him and for him alone. She knew he loved her beyond anything, more than anyone in the world, but only for his own sake; she was in his holy service.' This sounds like a confession. Possibly he was thinking of Mercedes when he wrote it.

Everything Florentino does after Fermina's marriage is based on the hope that he will hear news of her husband's death. A letter from her (full of insults) gives him the opportunity to write to her again.

In the letters, Fermina discovers a new Florentino, whom she likes better. Her ruminations on life and old age help her to survive her husband's death and to look to life with hope. She allows Florentino to visit on Tuesday afternoons. When her daughter reproaches her, Fermina explodes:

> **A century ago, they messed up my life with that poor man because they thought we were too young, and now they want to do it again because we are too old. They can go to hell. If we widows have anything going for us, it is that there's nobody to order us around anymore.**

Fermina and Florentino began their voyage of love aboard the *New Fidelity* and...

> **...they had lived together long enough to know that love was love at any time and in any place, but it became more solid the closer it came to death.**

The story has a happy ending: the novel concludes with the idea that the riverboat would continue to come and go, with the lovers on board, not only for the rest of their lives, but forever.

The Film School

An old dream of Gabo's came true in 1986 when the **Foundation for New Latin American Cinema** was created and he became its president. With his friend **Fernando Birri** he set up the **Film School** in Cuba. They had met thirty years before in Rome, when Birri had helped García Márquez find his way in the world of Italian film making. They had become close friends and had discussed the future of films in Latin America and dreamed of the possibility of working together. After six years at the school, Birri said: 'It was created in Cuba, the weakest country economically but with the strongest political and cultural will.'

Every year, García Márquez directed a workshop on writing for films. Ten young people would gather round a table to invent a story from scratch.

Gabo was in his element and these workshops became an addiction. He took the best students to Mexico to a professional workshop. There, they made television scripts for the commercial market and so earned money for the Foundation and the School.

In 1995 the *Film Workshop Series* was published, edited by García Márquez. Two books reproduced the author's talks with the members of his scriptwriting workshop in Cuba. In 'How to Tell a Story', the idea is to make up a story that can be told in a half-hour format. The author had an urge to teach, a willingness to share his own experience of writing fiction. He was not overbearing. He preferred dialogue, debate, a question or a suggestion to guide the process of creation within a group. The secrets of narration, the art of writing for films, and the magic of directing and producing are some of the themes of the book.

ADVICE FOR WRITERS

There's nothing worse than lengthening a story in an arbitrary way. If you cannot tell your story on one page, it either has something in excess or lacks something.

You shouldn't write about things you haven't a clue about, or that you don't feel personally.

You've got to have faith in any original concept that tells you something; if it speaks to you, far more often than not, it's sure to contain something.

Even when everybody believes something is good, you should be able to question it. It's not easy. But if you realise that something doesn't work in the story, is unsettling the structure, contradicts the character's personality, goes off at a tangent... well, then you've got to tear it up, even if it breaks your heart...

When you've got a story under way, you can't allow contradictory ideas to drag you off course: either we defend our stories or we give in to the temptation of turning them into different stories.

ADVICE FOR WRITERS

You've got to know where the limits of the believable lie—they're broader than you imagine. It's like playing chess. You establish with the spectator—or the reader—the rules of the game. As long as these are accepted, they cannot be broken; if you try to change them in the middle of the game, the other player will not accept it.

Inside the story, you have to establish categories, as in boxing. You must always work on your projects as if they were heavyweights, as if they need to have the punch of a heavyweight.

There's no real creation without risk and, thus, a measure of uncertainty. I never read my books again once they're published because I'm afraid to find defects in them that may have escaped notice. When I see the number of copies sold and the complimentary things the critics say, I'm afraid to discover that they're all wrong—critics and readers—and that the book is really shit... This dose of insecurity is terrible but, at the same time, necessary to produce something worthwhile. The arrogant ones who know it all, who are never in doubt, crash headlong to their death.

The inventiveness of reality has no limits. But you do run out of dramatic situations quickly. There are only three great dramatic situations: Life, Love and Death. The rest all fit into those.

'I Sell My Dreams' brings together the sixteen 'creative sessions' which covered the devising and writing of a script. With the help of the Brazilian film maker **Doc Comparato**, the workshop members were asked to write a script from the story of a woman who arrives at a house, offers her services as a dreamer and eliminates the members of the family. Before that script, 'I Sell My Dreams' had been a news article and one of the stories in *Strange Pilgrims*. There is an interesting exchange between Gabo and Doc:

I have no doubt about the identity of Alma. She can be very much like the one who died in the earthquake. She could be, but she's not.

Alma could have died in the earthquake and yet still be around making mischief.

But that's not her identity.

For me, it is. If you like, the detective discovers that there are 17 women with the same identity who died in the 1957 earthquake.

I like that.

You don't accept one miracle, but you do accept seventeen.

The thing is, she's a 'living dead' person.

She's not 'living dead'! You've made that up. She's herself.

Yes, but if she died and is called Alma (soul), she can levitate, walk through walls, and her fight with Amparo won't be real.

People only die forever in real life. In literature you can do what you like. That's why fiction was invented, so that you can get all your desires off your chest...

True... but Gabo, it's a script.

Those rationalist limitations terrify me, because they mean we can't do anything. Not even the thing with the dreams!

Driven by the memory of his youthful journeys, García Márquez wanted to write the story of the Magdalena River. The best excuse for telling it was Simon Bolívar's journey toward death. ***The General in His Labyrinth***, published in 1989, was this story from the life of the great South American general who died in 1830. It stemmed from a sentence:

> **After a long and hard journey on the Magdalena River, he died in Santa Marta, abandoned by his friends.**

José Palacios, his servant, finds him floating in the bath, naked and with his eyes open, and thinks he had drowned.

The entire novel turns on this sentence. It attempts to complete an episode that historians never spelled out. 'That's where the whole secret of the disaster the country is living is to be found', García Márquez says.

With each battle that Bolívar won, his skin was portrayed by artists as becoming lighter and lighter until he looked like a Roman. García Márquez studied the portraits carefully, but could not accept them as the image of the Liberator. He found a clue in a quotation from Bolívar's youth: 'I will die poor and naked'. *The General in His Labyrinth* builds on this image of nakedness, 'when glory had left his body.' At 47, Bolívar resigned the presidency of Colombia and embarked on his final journey.

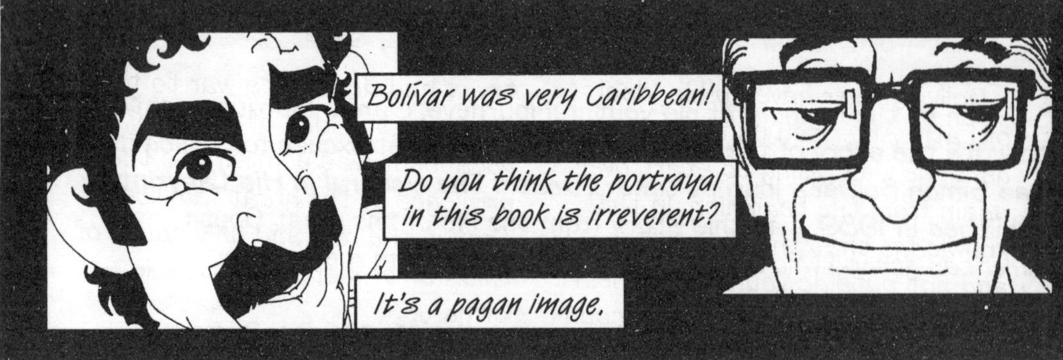

As he immersed himself in the character, he realised that it had nothing to do with the Bolívar taught in school. He wanted to show the man behind the bronze image, to demythologise him. As a typical Caribbean man, his Bolívar wanders about naked, a prey to insomnia, and is passionate about dancing and women. From the many women in Bolívar's life, he calls our attention to **Manuela Sáenz**, the spirited Quiteña, with whom he maintained an ardent love affair for eight years. The book took three years to research and two to write. He wrote nine versions, revised by Venezuelan historians. *The General in His Labyrinth* showed that all of García Márquez's writing is related to the same geographical and historical contexts.

The journey was the least documented part of Bolívar's life. García Márquez portrayed the general absorbed in the magic of the river, dying and defeated, but with his dignity intact. Though the novel form gave him the freedom to invent, there is not a single historical fact that was not confirmed. The book was written like a contemporary chronicle.

Bolívar never gave up his ideal of Latin American unity. In Cartagena, he was willing to start over again from the beginning, in the knowledge that the enemy is inside and not outside your own home. He said: 'The oligarchies of each country… had declared a war to the death on the idea of integrity, because it was contrary to the privileges of the great families. That is the real and only cause of this war of dispersion that is killing us.'

In this book there are echoes of *No One Writes to the Colonel*, but this story has a firm historical base. The characters are, however, quite similar. To abandonment, deterioration, solitude, they oppose their hope. Moral grandeur is as important to both of them as their chronic constipation. This fact alone is enough to define their characters.

It was inevitable that the writer would project himself into his characters—especially the main one. Gabo identified with the hero in that the idea of death should not distract him from what he was doing in life. He loaned Bolívar his rage, which the general managed as well as he himself did. And he explored his relationships with women. He has Bolívar say:

> *I'll never fall in love again. It's like having two souls at the same time.*

On 10 December 1830, the general is so ill when he wakes up that the bishop has to be called in urgently. After a brief confession behind closed doors, the bishop leaves quickly, without saying goodbye and looking upset. He does not conduct the subsequent funeral service nor is he present at the burial. The general speaks to Doctor Révérend.

Recycling Stories

García Márquez sees no distinction between his work in literature, journalism or films. They are all means to tell stories about people. He only feels well when he is working; even his ulcer disappears then.

In the introduction to *Strange Pilgrims: Twelve Stories* (1992) he referred to the these stories as '...a collection of short stories, based on events reported in the newspapers but redeemed from their mortal condition by the cunning of poetry.' He spent eighteen years writing them, losing them, then writing them again.

When he began the *Chronicle of a Death Foretold* he learned that even in the intervals between books he would lose the habit of writing, and that each time it was harder to take it up again. Because of this, between 1980 and 1984 he made himself write a weekly article for papers in a number of countries, as a discipline to keep his writing hand in working order (and this earned him fees comparable to those earned by famous footballers and boxers). A selection of these articles appears in **Press Notes** (1991).

The stories are fictionalised reminiscences of his adventures in Europe, accounts of the strange things that happen to Latin Americans there. Before publishing them, he returned to the principal locations: Barcelona, Geneva, Rome and Paris. He rewrote all the stories.

None of them was now anything like what I remembered. They had all been rarefied through an astonishing inversion: the real memories felt like ghosts of memory, while the false memories were so convincing that they had supplanted reality. It was impossible for me to see the line between disappointment and nostalgia. I had found what I needed to finish the book: a point of view through time.

For eight feverish months I never had to ask myself where reality left off and imagination began, because I was aided by the suspicion that possibly nothing I had experienced in Europe twenty-five years before was true.

Yesterday I dreamed of you. You must leave right away and not come back to Vienna for the next five years.

With all his Caribbean superstitions to the fore, he never returned.

Another story recreates a situation lived in Cadaqués, where he used to spend the summer, until he had a bad omen. He experienced the *tramontana*—a terrible wind that puts one on edge—and decided that if he came out of there alive, he would never return.

In the introductory note to the book, he revealed the specifics of writing.

- The effort required to write a short story is as intense as beginning a novel.
- In the novel's first paragraph, one must define everything: structure, tone, style, rhythm, length and even some of the character's personality. The rest is the pleasure of writing, the most intimate and solitary that exists, and if one does not continue to correct the book for the rest of one's life, it is because the same iron rigour that was needed to start the book is applied to finishing it.
- Any version of a story is better than the preceding one. How can one tell which will be the last? This is a professional secret, a matter for the magic of instinct, just like a cook knowing when the soup is done.

Speaking of magic, *One Hundred Years of Solitude* will never be made into a film—the magical dialectic of the written word will not be seen on the screen. Despite the enormous sums of money offered for it—the most recent being two million dollars—the idea spooks him. Gabo understands the limitations of film. He knows that the work of the novelist is the freest there is.

I want readers to continue imagining the characters just the way they visualise them. In film the image is so defined that the viewer cannot imagine the character the way he likes, but only the way the screen makes him see.

The film director Luis Buñuel used to say:

From a great writer one must choose a little-known, minor work, and add whatever the narrator left out. A masterpiece hardly allows this. It's only possible to make it worse.

While Gabo thought about his next novel, he worked on three television series and as many full-length films. He also tried to write his memoirs.

I don't know if they're going to disappoint. People expect me to tell the political and military secrets of my friends who are presidents, like Fidel Castro. But Fidel and I spend our time talking about books and food!

The memoirs will tell how he educated himself to be a writer, and of his childhood, journalism, his friends, his years in Europe and his desire to live many lives.

There's no reason to say anything about my private life. I'm very reticent about that. I won't be able to prevent others talking about the role I played in their lives. And they will tell—not just the men, but the women, too.

His intimate life can be best understood by reading his books. It is all there. Further explanations annoy him.

Of Love and Other Demons (1994) tells of the romance of a twelve-year-old Creole countess, and a thirty-year-old priest who has read too much about hell. The style, language and characters are reminiscent of *One Hundred Years of Solitude.*

Gabo adores symmetry. On the one hand is Sierva María, the daughter of a marquis and a mestiza who is abandoned by her parents and reared in the slave quarters. She embodies the pagan world of African tongues and deities. On the other hand is Cayetano Delaura, a theologian in the service of the bishop, who belongs to the white and Catholic world of the European colonists. The novel's strength lies in the author's desire to give equal weight to the effect of these opposite poles.

In the prologue, García Márquez invented a source for his story. He claimed that in 1949 he had been sent to the ancient Convent of Santá Clara de Cartagena to look for a news story. The funeral crypts were being emptied, and there he 'found' the novel's main character when the remains of a twelve-year-old girl with a head of hair twenty-two metres, eleven centimetres long were discovered. Her headstone gave the name Sierva María de Todos los Angeles.

The real basis for the story came from his research for *Love in the Time of Cholera*. An episode in Daniel Lemaitre's *History of Cartagena* recounted a quarrel between the Capuchins and the Clarissas, which centred on the love of one of the governor's lieutenants for a novice. The setting was the mythical slave-owning Cartagena of the 18th century.

Of Love and Other Demons

An ash-coloured dog with a star on its forehead broke into the market, on the first Sunday in December, overturned tables of fried innards, dismembered the Indians tents and the lottery stands, and in passing bit four people who crossed its path. Three were black slaves. The other was Sierva María de Todos los Angeles, only daughter of the Marquis of Casalduero, who had gone with a servant to buy a string of bells for her twelfth birthday party.

In the port a cargo of slaves is being auctioned. The maid chats with Bernarda, Sierva's mother, about the scandal in the port. Bernarda has been an astute slave trader until 'she had been erased from the world through her abuse of mead and cacao tablets'.

A party is being held in the slaves' courtyard to celebrate Sierva María's twelfth birthday:

> **In that oppressive world where no one was free, Sierva María was free: only she, and only there... In her real house with her real family... She danced with more grace and spirit than the Africans, sang in voices not her own in the different languages of Africa, or with the voices of birds and animals.**

When her father, the marquis, discovers that Sierva María has been bitten in the market by a rabid dog, he meets Abrenuncio, 'the most notable and controversial doctor in the city. 'A Portuguese Jew with the terrifying speciality of predicting to those who were ill the day and hour of their death.' The marquis asks him to visit his daughter. Abrenuncio says that his daughter knew that the dog was mad.

The marquis points out that the girl has told ingenious lies.

Her heart told me. She was like a small caged frog.

Perhaps she'll be a poet.

The more transparent the writing, the more you see the poetry.

The marquis appeals to other doctors, healers and sorcerers. Even the most audacious abandon the girl, convinced that she is mad or possessed by a demon. The bishop proposes sending her away to the Convent of Santa Clara because of her 'unmistakable symptoms of demonic possession'. He appoints Father Cayetano Delaura to be her exorcist, but Cayetano has had a premonitory dream. In the dream it was clear that:

> **The girl had spent many years in front of that infinite window trying to finish the bunch of grapes, and was in no hurry, for she knew that in the last grape lay death.**

Far from finding her possessed, Cayetano discovers in her his own 'disease'. He visits her every afternoon, improves the conditions of her captivity and brings her sweets. Cayetano recites verses from Garcilaso de la Vega, such as those Gabito had learned in school.

One day, Sierva tells him that she has seen snow in a dream, the same one he had dreamed. She becomes upset when he tells her that her father wants to visit her. When he tries to loosen the strap around her ankle, she becomes so angry that the priest witnesses 'the dreadful spectacle of a possessed soul'.

Cayetano flees. He shuts himself in the library, to pray and weep. 'He opened Sierva's little case and placed the things on the table. He got to know them, smelled them with an avid bodily desire, loved them, spoke to them in obscene hexameters, until he could bear no more.'

He began to flagellate himself with an insatiable hatred that would not stop until he had extirpated from his soul even the last vestige of Sierva María.

After hearing his confession, the bishop sends him to nurse the hospital's lepers. But Cayetano, mad with love for Sierva María, returns by night to the convent through a secret passageway and declares his love to Sierva María.

Night after night, 'they wore themselves out in kisses, uttered the poetry of love through tears, sang into one another's ear, tossed in a swamp of desire to the limit of their strength: exhausted but virgin.' After a prisoner escapes, the passageway is walled up but Sierva never discovers why Cayetano does not return to her cell. Under the Inquisition, Cayetano is condemned to continue working in the hospital, 'where he lived for many years with his diseased patients without achieving his wish of contracting leprosy'. After several sessions of exorcism, Sierva again dreams of the snow-covered countryside and the grapes. This time she plucked them two by two, anxious to gain the very last grape from the bunch.

The guard who came in to prepare her for the sixth session of exorcism found her dead of love sickness in the bed with her eyes radiant and her skin like a new-born's. Clumps of hair sprouted as they grew back on her shaven head.

Literary Carpentry

García Márquez routinely throws out all his notes and documentation and destroys all rough drafts of his books so that no vestiges remain.

The way he works is the most intimate part of his private life.

He did break the habit, however, with *Of Love and Other Demons*. He showed his wife eleven versions. One page of these drafts showed his obsession with reaching a perfection of style.

He is very protective of his relationship with the mystery of his craft: 'if a critic were to read these drafts, he would know the lies I have told and the things I have made up, and I don't want to be known in this way.' In any event, originals corrected by his own hand are now worth more than the books themselves.

Since the end of the 1970s when a friend sold some of his personal letters to an American university, he stopped writing them. To communicate with friends he uses the phone, at an astronomical cost. He is both meticulous and superstitious. He has one absolute rule: wherever he is, he writes a page every day. And he always makes two copies: one on paper and one on disk.

While still in bed, at five in the morning he checks the pages he left on the table the night before. The only exception is when he has to take a plane. Then he allows several days' work to pile up beforehand. Keeping busy during the flight is an efficient way to distract himself from his congenital fear of flying. He says: 'The principle that I have set myself as a writer is self-criticism. Revising my work gives me much pleasure.'

Writing itself is relatively easy for him. 'When I sit down to write the first sentence, I have the complete story in my head. I also need to know the names of all the characters before I begin. After that, it all flows with no blocks,' he says. The shelves of his study are filled with reference books. When he needs to kill off a character and doesn't know how, he has to hand detailed instructions for the perfect crime.

A novelist must have knowledge of many fields.

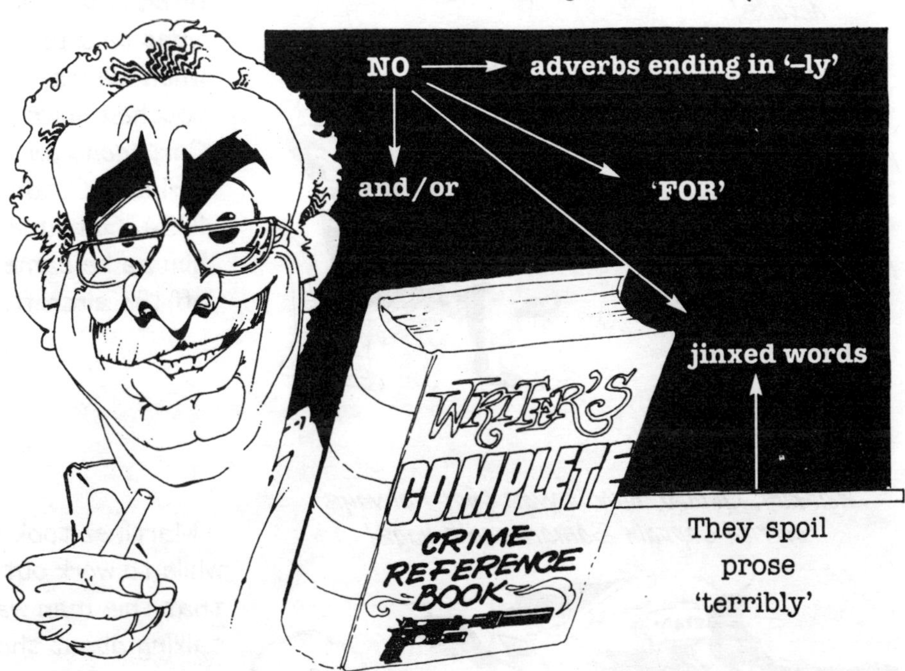

When he reaches the end and has solved the narrative structure, he continues to improve the text. 'I alternate: sometimes I work on the rhythm, at other times on the language. I also have to clear up all the grammatical issues I may have.' Though he does say that he is now 'a bit less obsessive', he aims at a perfect structure (each chapter must have the same number of pages), and perfect language (he cannot bear to use the same adjective twice in a book).

The Best Job in The World

What García Márquez misses most about journalism is the doing of it. He would like to discover everything, but finds that he soon becomes the news himself. A measure of anonymity is necessary for the job of reporter, and that is impossible for him. He spoke to Tomas Eloy Martínez of his desire to...

...jointly found a workshop for journalism. I've already worked out all the details!

I have no right to refuse to explain what I have learned in a nearly completed life.

Martínez agreed to meet with Gabo a month later, not knowing what to expect when his plane touched down in Cartagena de Indias in October 1994. Gabo met him as he came off the aircraft.

Tell him, Gabito, how it was that I always carried Captain Samaritano's bags!

Martínez took a while to work out that this man was talking about the captain of the steamer *New Fidelity* in *Love in the Time of Cholera*. In Colombia, Gabo is something of a national treasure.

To walk with Gabo through the streets of the walled city, one of the most beautiful in the world, is nearly impossible. Whenever he returns to his own country, discreet security follows him everywhere.

The Fundacion para el Nuevo Periodismo Iberoamericano (Foundation for New Iberian American Journalism) was sponsored by UNESCO and fifteen newspapers from Latin America, Spain and the United States. Among its well-known teachers are Gay Talese, Claudio Magris, Robert Darnton and Norman Mailer, along with a rotating roster of colleagues who are specialists in different areas of the profession. The idea is to transmit experience the old way.

From its creation in 1995, the 'school without walls' gathered young newsmen together in workshops, seminars and courses on topics that schools of journalism usually leave out. In his workshops on narration, Gabo generally started with a joke, to break the ice.

In the flood of anecdotes, he always managed to transmit the secrets of what he calls 'the best job in the world'.

- Reporting is the story of what happened, a literary genre assigned to journalism, for which you must be a narrator dedicated to reality.
- As a reporter, you can write whatever you want, with two conditions: that you do so in a credible way, and that you know in your conscience that what you are writing is true.
- Journalism is mechanical, there are nuts and bolts whose use you have to learn. You've got to have professional pride.
- You have to believe in what you're doing. The reporter's boredom is the reader's boredom.
- There are ethical onslaughts to be faced that result from the notion of the intrepid nature of the job, based on sanctifying the idea of 'getting the scoop at any cost'. People who do this are not moved by the notion that the best news is not always the first to appear, but that which is presented in the best way.
- The journalist's first duty is to be wary of the source. Often you can become an unwitting instrument.
- Nowadays newsrooms are usually laboratories for solitary navigators, where it seems easier to communicate with the movements of the stars than with the hearts of readers. There's galloping dehumanisation at work.

MORE ADVICE

- How do you begin? Think of the anecdote that had the greatest impact on you, and start with that. It's hard, but it's always good.
- A good story is like a sausage. You have to tie up the end and then stuff everything in, and allow nothing to fall out. It will be a good story if you know where you're headed before you sit down to write.
- You have to tell the story as if the reader had been there. It doesn't matter what the reader forgets: when he reaches the end, he'll remember the beginning.
- The end is as important as the beginning. If you get the reader to read the last paragraph, you will have won most of the battle. But if there's no closing, the reader will think, 'So I read this far for this?'
- Journalism is a trap. Whoever is really caught up in it never escapes.
- To be a journalist you must have a vocation, and having a vocation is the only human condition that has ever defeated love.

He never allowed tape recorders in the classrooms. Gabo was as intent on escaping from them as he was from the rigours of an interview. In *Press Notes*, he summed up his objections to the genre:

When you have to give, on average, an interview a month for twelve years, you end up developing a special kind of imagination, so they won't all be repetitions of the same interview... The interview long ago abandoned the rigorous boundaries of journalism to become a pirate operation in the mangroves of fiction.

In his workshops, there was time for dancing and socialising. Someone asked him why he returned to Colombia if his life there was in danger.

> You fly into Bogotá's spooky airport and promise yourself that it will be the last time. But in the evening you see your friends, and the first drink brings a certain peace. The second makes you think things are not so bad, and after the third glass, my friends, Colombia is one of the best countries in the entire world.

He has also said that he lacks the time to make a 'serious' return to Buenos Aires and that he is afraid of destroying the memory of 'the only perfect fortnight of my life'. Rumour has it that he believes he will die there.

Toward the end of 1995, as he was sending off the proofs of **News of a Kidnapping**, an exemplary report on the everyday drama of Colombians, he received a call. The husband of Maruja Pachón, one of the book's main characters, was on the phone. They spoke of another kidnapping, that of Juan Carlos Gaviria, the former president's brother. The kidnappers had sent a letter to the media: they wanted Gabo to take the place of the then President Ernesto Samper.

A similar message had earlier been sent by Subcomandante Marcos, the leader of the Mexican Zapatista rebels. It had received the following reply:

No one can expect me to be so irresponsible as to become the worst president of the Republic.

He sent an emphatic message to the kidnappers:

Free Gaviria, bury your weapons and go out and promote your ideas of renewal under the protection of a new constitutional order.

For García Márquez, the great problem of Latin America is the lack of identity, with one exception: Cuba. His support for the Cuban revolution—and Castro—is unconditional. Dozens of times, he has used his voice and influence to attempt to get the US embargo of Cuba lifted. At other times, he has used his friendship with Castro to make it possible for the regime's political prisoners to leave the island.

News of a Kidnapping took three years to write. In eleven chapters and an epilogue of identical length he tells the facts in an alternating way: the odd-numbered chapters explain what is happening with the kidnapped group; the even-numbered ones show what is happening on the outside.

There's no flirtation with Joyce in this. The best recipe for stories is to tell them straight. What this construction requires of me is the right theme.

From the first sentence, the book grabs the reader's attention:

Before getting into the car, she looked over her shoulder to be certain that no one was following her. It was five past seven in the evening in Bogotá. Night had fallen an hour earlier, the Parque Nacional was badly lit and the leafless trees cast a ghostly profile on to the murky and hapless sky, but there was not anything to fear in sight.

In three years of work, Gabo had been to hundreds of meetings and interviews, deciphered 120 cassettes and studied thousands of press reports and documents. The book tells the story of nine kidnappings—of eight journalists and a politician's sister—carried out by drug lord Pablo Escobar's henchmen between August 1990 and June 1991 as a way of pressuring the government of César Gaviria.

I imagined how the life of each one of the kidnap victims was going, what the lives of the victims' families were like and I showed to what extent this situation affected the entire country. The facts of the book are so extraordinary that it looks more like a novel than all my novels. Incredible things happened.

In life, García Márquez makes less of a distinction between reality and fiction than he does in his books. His life has many fantastic ingredients.

People don't observe themselves in that way. Extraordinary things happen around them but they don't perceive them. I think there's another reality, or a wider reality than we imagine. You don't have to go round finding a logical explanation for everything.

That is the essence of his life. The conversations he has nowadays with his mother are somewhat delirious. Since 1992, the entire García Márquez clan gets together to celebrate the New Year, and the wit of 'Miss Luisa', who at 94 vacillates between a wandering mind and implacable lucidity.

In an attempt to rescue a past that keeps the entire family up at nights, Gabo instigated a number of family reunions. Whenever they get together, they rescue some story from their treasure chest and they all recycle it.

For García Márquez, the 'secret of longevity and happiness is to do only that which you enjoy'. There has never been a Nobel Prize winner who wrote as much as he did, and he believes that he has only been able to write because Mercedes 'carried the world on her shoulders'.

The purging of style in *News of a Kidnapping* awoke in him the strong desire to write fiction again.

He began working on three books, all pure inventions. The first has its point of departure in the story 'House of the Sleeping Beauties', by Yasumari Kawabata about the ancient bourgeoisie of Kyoto. Another rescues a minor character from *Love in the Time of Cholera*, don Rodrigo de Buen Lozano, a Spanish viceroy who was brought back to life by love.

The third tells the story of a man who will die at the end. From the moment he began writing it—around the end of 1994—he has had the strange feeling that when he types the final full stop, he will suffer a fate identical to that of his hero. That is why he has written only two chapters in four years.

This damned novel	Death is a woman who waits patiently for him until his task is done.	This damned novel

In January 1999, García Márquez surprised us once again. He took pleasure in being part of a group that purchased the Colombian weekly magazine **Cambio 16**. He continues to have a hand in everything. When the preliminary peace talks between the government of **President Andrés Pastrana** and the **Revolutionary Armed Forces of Colombia** (the FARC) began, Gabo went to cover the meeting as one of the magazine's reporters.

At the party to celebrate *Cambio's* renaissance, Gabo stayed until midnight, greeting the two thousand guests. When he returned to the office, he remained there all night, working on a long article on the new president of Venezuela, **Hugo Chávez**. As the sun came up, just before the deadline...

It was only the beginning. He has returned to journalism, making the dream of his fellow journalists come true. He has again flown frequently, sending articles from Paris, Madrid, Rome, now as a celebrity correspondent. He enthusiastically attended the première of *No One Writes to the Colonel* and looks forward to the film of, *The Autumn of the Patriarch* with Marlon Brando in the title role. Even though his doctors made him check in to a Bogotá clinic to recover from 'exhaustion', Gabito refuses to rest. But, for how long? Melquíades answers for him: 'To the end!'

Bibliography

WORKS BY GABRIEL GARCÍA MÁRQUEZ

Leaf Storm (1955)
No One Writes to the Colonel (1959)
Big Mama's Funeral (1961)
In Evil Hour (1962)
One Hundred Years of Solitude (1967)
Isabel Watching it Rain in Macondo (1967)
Eyes of a Blue Dog (1968)
The Story of a Shipwrecked Sailor (1970)
The Incredible and Sad Tale of Innocent Eréndira and Her Heartless Grandmother (1972)
The Autumn of the Patriarch (1975)
Operation Carlota (1978)
Ninety Days Behind the Iron Curtain (1979)
Costeño Texts (1981)
Chronicle of a Death Foretold (1981)
Among Cachacos I & II (1982)
Clandestine in Chile: The Adventures of Miguel Littín (1985)
Love in the Time of Cholera (1985)
The General in His Labyrinth (1989)
Press Notes 1980-1984 (1991)
Strange Pilgrims: Twelve Stories (1992)
Of Love and Other Demons (1994)
Diatriba de amor contra un hombre sentado (1995)
The Smell of Guava: Conversations with Plinio Apuleyo (1995)
News of a Kidnapping (1996)
For the Sake of a Country Within Reach of the Children (1998)

WORKS AND IDEAS OF GARCÍA MÁRQUEZ MADE INTO FILMS

Time to Die (Arturo Ripstein, 1964)
María of My Heart (Jaime Hermosillo, 1978)
Eréndira (Ruy Guerra, 1982)
Chronicle of a Death Foretold (Francesco Rossi, 1987)
A Very Old Gentleman with Enormous Wings (1988)
Difficult Loves (1987-1988)
I Sell My Dreams (1992)
Oedipus the Mayor (with Jorge Ali Triana, 1987)

No One Writes to the Colonel (Arturo Ripstein, 1999)
The Autumn of the Patriarch (Sean Penn, 2000)

BOOKS ABOUT GARCÍA MÁRQUEZ

Bell, Michael, *Gabriel García Márquez: Solitude and Solidarity*, St. Martins Press, 1993

Bell-Villada, Gene H., *García Márquez: The Man and His Work*, University of North Carolina Press, 1990

Bloom, Harold (ed), *Gabriel García Márquez*, Chelsea House Publishers, 1992

Clark, Gloria Jeanne Bodtorf, *A Synergy of Styles: Art and Artefact in Gabriel García Márquez*, University Press of America, 1999

Fiddian, Robin W., *García Márquez (Modern Literature in Perspective)*, Pearson Education, 1995

James, Regina, *Gabriel García Márquez: Revolutions in Wonderland*, University of Missouri Press, 1981

McGuirak, Bernard & Cardwell, Richard (eds), *Gabriel García Márquez: New Readings*, Cambridge University Press, 1987

McMurray, G.R., *Gabriel García Márquez: Life, Work, and Criticism*, York Press, 1987

Mellen, Joan, *Literary Masters: Gabriel García Márquez*, Gale Group, 2000

Rodriguez-Vergara, Isabel, *Haunting Demons: Critical Essays on the Works of García Márquez*, Columbus Memorial Library, 1998

Sims, Robert L., *Evolution of Myth in García Márquez from La Hojarasca to Cien Anos De Soledad*, Ediciones Universal, 1982

Williams, Raymond L., *Gabriel García Márquez*, Twayne, 1984

Index

The Authors

Mariana Solanet is an Argentinian journalist and translator. She studied Journalism and Arts while working as a tour guide and English teacher. She has worked for the Buenos Aires daily newspaper **La Nación**. She has also translated the Argentinian editions of **Che For Beginners, Gestalt For Beginners** and **Sai Baba For Beginners** into English.

Hector Luis Bergandi is an Argentinian artist who specialises in illustrations, sketches and paintings of automobiles, for which he has gained international recognition. His 'trademark' works have, for 20 years, appeared in **Road & Truck**. At times, he takes a break, as with this book, which lets him return to his recurring theme with renewed vigour.

Thanks to the staff at Alfguara and Norma y Sudamericana publishers, and to the library and archives of La Nación for the books and articles which have helped in this work; to Waldo Casal for the astrological profile of GGM; to Eduardo Caraballa for the shared music and other (Caribbean) stuff; to JCK for his confidence and encouragement. This book is dedicated to José and to my children, Lucas and Guido.

– M.S.